"S　　　　　　　　　　　　　　**ady
to p**　　　　　　　　　　　　**ze.**

Sa　　　　　　　　　　　　　　ated
"On　　　　　　　　　　　　　　re-
ques　　　　　　　　, steadily, the Jeep began
to rock. Suddenly it roared out of the bog onto
solid ground, and Sam gave a cry of triumph.
Mercy shouted, too, and he turned, then
groaned to see her sitting on her rear in the
swamp. "I'm coming," he called to Mercy, who
was yelling for help. But first he took off his
boots and his watch, and rolled up his jeans.
"Be right there!"

Mercy subsided into stunned silence. Why
hadn't he rushed to her rescue? "Are you sure
you don't want to run home and get your
bathing suit? I don't mind marinating here
until you get back."

Sam gave her a sweet smile. "Patience,
angel. I know exactly what to do." He picked
his way through the mud until he was close
enough for Mercy to put out her hand. He
took it, but instead of pulling her to her feet,
he kissed the tips of her fingers. "Accept my
apologies for this incident," he said. Then,
without warning, he threw himself face first
into the marsh.

"You're crazy!" she yelped. "Sam, are you
okay?"

After a moment, he sat up, moss on his
nose and chin, a water lily over one ear. "I
know women," he said. "They demand equality. It's easier to get slimed myself than suffer
the guilt of being dry and clean."

Mercy burst out laughing. "You don't leave
anything to chance, do you?"

He pulled her to him, and gave her his
pirate's grin. "Not this time. . . ."

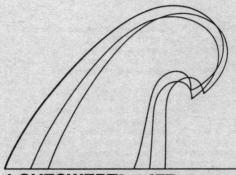

LOVESWEPT® • 477

Tonya Wood

Gorgeous

 BANTAM BOOKS
NEW YORK • TORONTO • LONDON • SYDNEY • AUCKLAND

GORGEOUS

A Bantam Book / June 1991

If you would be interested in receiving protective vinyl
covers for your Loveswept books, please write to this address
for information:

Loveswept
Bantam Books
P.O. Box 985
Hicksville, NY 11802

ISBN 0-553-44105-1

Published simultaneously in the United States and Canada

Bantam Books are published by Bantam Books, a division
of Bantam Doubleday Dell Publishing Group, Inc. Its trademark, consisting of the words "Bantam Books" and the
portrayal of a rooster, is Registered in U.S. Patent and
Trademark Office and in other countries. Marca Registrada.
Bantam Books, 666 Fifth Avenue, New York, New York
10103.

PRINTED IN THE UNITED STATES OF AMERICA

OPM   0 9 8 7 6 5 4 3 2 1

One

All he wanted was aspirin.

He would be in and out of the drugstore in two minutes flat and he'd leave his car parked in the fire lane for a quick getaway. He figured he could get away with it.

Sam Christie drove his Jeep Renegade up and over the curb in front of The Circle K, barely missing the newspaper stand and coming to a stop two inches from the fire hydrant. He hadn't meant to end up on the sidewalk, but his fever was climbing steadily and his depth perception was a little off. Also his eyes were watering, his muscles were quivering, and his headache was so painful, it hurt to think. For a man cut down in his prime by a nasty flu bug, he thought he'd done an admirable job of parking.

He tugged his baseball cap low over his eyes and turned up the collar of his shirt. Some-where in the back of his stewed brain, flashed the image of Humphrey Bogart pulling up the collar of his trenchcoat to be inconspicuous. The colorful Rugby shirt Sam wore was less effective, but every little bit helped. He got out of the car and walked into the store, trying to look nonchalant. The air conditioning hit his feverish skin like a subzero hurricane, and the chills intensified. He noticed a middle-aged woman in a neon-pink jogging suit staring at him with a peculiar expression, and he forced himself to walk faster. He speed-wobbled to the aisle with cold remedies and painkillers and grabbed a bottle of aspirin, then to the Icee drink dispenser for a jumbo grape Tummybuster. He realized that he was being trailed at an indiscreet distance by the woman in neon pink, and he made a beeline to the front counter as fast as his spaghetti legs could carry him. There were two people ahead of him in line, just his bad luck, he thought. Perspiration began to break out on his brow, and he leaned against the magazine rack for support. Lately the most uncomfortable things had been happening to him in checkout lines.

"Excuse me?"

Someone tapped him on the shoulder. Twisting his neck, which creaked like a rusty spring, Sam glanced at the woman behind him. His pink shadow. "Yes?"

"I can't believe it." She slapped both hands on her cheeks, her eyes wide and growing wider. "You're standing right here in front of me! I knew you lived here in Denver, but I never thought I'd actually meet you. My word, it's really you!"

Not only was her booming, Ethel-Merman voice attracting a great deal of attention, but it was aggravating the demon throbbing under his skull. "I think you've made a mistake," he said slurring his vowels heavily. "I'm not me. I mean, you've confused me with someone else."

She wasn't listening. She grabbed the latest issue of a magazine from the rack, her bright-eyed gaze swinging from the glossy cover to Sam and back again. "There you are, right on the cover. 'Sam Christie, Rebel Without a Pause'! Somebody pinch me!"

The clerk stopped checking. The elderly woman in front of Sam put on her bifocals and zeroed in on him. Other people were gathering around the checkstand, a blurry mosaic of bright colors and excited voices. Sam wondered how long his poor legs would support him.

"My Icee is melting," he mumbled.

"Would you mind giving me your auto-graph?" the woman in pink asked, waving the magazine in front of his face. "Write some-thing across the cover, and make it to Audrey Krantz. My husband isn't going to believe I actually met you. He fancies himself quite a skier, but, of course, he's nothing compared to you. Imagine, an Olympic gold medalist! I'll never forget that news conference of yours a few years ago, before you raced in the down-hill. There you sat, cool as a cucumber, as you promised America a gold medal. Doyle said you were cocky."

Sam blinked at her. "Doyle?"

"My husband. He said you were cocky, but I said you were self-confident. I loved the way you had all that long hair tied back in a ponytail. Doyle said you were full of yourself. I said you were a free spirit."

"Doyle was right."

"Do you know, I won't buy him anything but Comfort Weave underwear, and it's because of the way you look in those magazine ads."

"I love the television commercial you did for that health spa," the elderly woman put in. "I'm not too old to appreciate a good body."

Sam felt very unwell and more than a little sorry for himself. He wanted to go home, but experience had taught him it was easier to give in gracefully. Moving in slow motion, he carefully set the aspirin and the Icee down on the counter, then took a pen from his pocket. Audrey handed him the magazine, and he scrawled an illegible greeting right across his own smiling, sun-browned face. Before he could put the pen away, someone gave him another copy of the magazine and asked him to write something to Katie—then there was Allison, then Cricket, then a gentleman named Knowlton, who wanted an autograph for his daughter, Peggy. Sam hardly heard one word out of ten that were spoken to him. By the time he escaped to his car, his hair was damp with perspiration, and the pain in his head seemed to have spread throughout his entire body. He ached everywhere, every weary limb, every stiff, burning joint. He washed down three aspirin with his grape Icee, wincing each time he swallowed. The air seemed to vibrate around him as he drove home, heating up as if coming from a furnace. It took an incredible amount of concentration for him to keep the Jeep on the road, particularly since a thunderstorm had come out of the west and his visibility was limited to the blinding glare of headlights through a sheet of water. When he finally pulled into the underground parking garage of his apartment building, he was shaking with sheer relief. Eleven floors up, in his wonderfully private, wonderfully quiet penthouse apartment, was his custom-made extra firm mattress with the built-in massager. There was no place like home, he thought.

Unfortunately, he still had to get from the basement to the top floor, and the elevator wouldn't cooperate. Sam repeatedly pushed the lights that sparkled on the control panel, but only succeeded in sending the elevator up and down like a yo-yo. His stomach had permanently lodged in his throat, and the Icee had splashed over the side of the cup and through his fingers by the time the doors opened on the tenth floor—but at least he had made some progress. Slowly, with childlike deliberation, he pressed the button for the top floor, sighing as the doors closed once again and the elevator lurched into motion. Sam was exhausted but triumphant. He leaned back against the wall, then watched with startled, fever-bright eyes as his feet slowly slipped from beneath him. It irritated him that he was going to pass out at this stage of the game. Why hadn't he thrown his drink away before he got into the elevator? He was going to spill grape goop all over his new shirt. He'd never get the stains out, never. . . .

His field of vision became blurred and distorted, quickly fading to a soft gray. Going . . . going . . .

Gone.

Mercy Rose Sullivan had the hiccups. She had received a telegram that had upset her, and whenever she was upset, she got, the hiccups. She put a paper sack over her head and tried to calm down. Usually it was the only way she could get rid of her nervous hiccups, breathing in carbon monoxide or dioxide or whatever it was a person breathed inside paper sacks. Unfortunately, these hiccups came from deep within her frustrated soul and were exceptionally stubborn. After five minutes she still wasn't cured, and she was feeling claustrophobic. She ripped off the sack, then tried holding her breath while she stood on her head. That didn't work either, and she collapsed in a dizzy, hiccupping bundle on the carpet.

And it was all because of that damn Yankee.

Mercy flopped over on her back, brown eyes narrowed as she stared at the photograph on the fireplace mantel. Sheer perfection was captured in that five-by-seven-inch frame, a green-eyed Adonis with molded cheekbones, a square jaw, a tiny cleft in his oh-so-manly chin. Deep creases framed a smile that was so white, so incredibly perfect, Mercy couldn't help but think back guiltily to the last time she'd gone to the dentist for a good cleaning. Thick dark hair curled up over the edges of a New York Yankees baseball cap, the effect boyish and endearing. His shoulders were as perfect as the rest of him, giving incredible shape to the gray baseball uniform he wore. Just looking at that apparition of male loveliness doubled the intensity of the hiccups. He was all-American. He was virile. He was disarming and charming.

He was coming to get her.

Mercy pressed her eyes closed tightly, then opened them again. "I'm in control here," she told the slow-moving ceiling fan. "I won't let Tucker Healy affect me—*hic*—this way. He's my *ex*-fiancé. My *ex*-Achilles heel. My ex-everything. What am I, a mature, independent woman or a helpless—*hic*—rabbit?"

She knew herself too well to answer that question. She wrapped her arms around her ribs, trying to hold herself together through another violent hiccup. No one, *no one* could get a paper bag over her head quicker than Tucker Healy. Ever since she was thirteen years old, she'd been suffering from Tucker-induced hiccups. He had been the light in her eyes and the thorn in her side; now, over ten years later, she wanted to believe things had changed. She wanted to believe she was no longer susceptible to his irrepressible "dog-ate-my-homework" charm. A broken heart and a broken engagement hadn't cured her. Putting two thousand miles between them hadn't cured her. Maybe someone ought to knock her over the head with a baseball bat. That surely would cure her.

She had to get out of the apartment. She was zipping right along into stage two of her personal crisis routine, which was a feeding frenzy. She jumped to her feet and ran to the front hall closet, tugging a shapeless khaki-green rain slicker over her faded cotton paja-mas. She rolled up her pantlegs, hiding the telltale rosebud print, then pulled on a pair of yellow vinyl boots. A floppy-brimmed plastic hat and a startling, hot-pink umbrella with an enamel goose-head handle completed her out-fit. In the midst of a personal crisis, one didn't worry about making a fashion statement. Besides, she only had twenty minutes before the German deli across the street closed. Right now, more than anything in the world, she needed a giant-size piece of their sinfully rich Black Forest cake, followed by a chaser of hot apple strudel. A terrific sugar rush would be just the thing to distract her from the calamity winging its way toward her on United flight 309.

Mercy's apartment was on the fourth floor, directly across the hall from the elevator. She had no intention of actually using the eleva-tor, however, since it made her feel even more claustrophobic than a paper sack. She locked her door, then hooked her umbrella over her arm and headed straight for the stairwell. She would never have noticed the shoe protruding from the elevator door if she hadn't tripped over it.

She stopped dead in her tracks, blinking twice. There was a white leather running shoe preventing the elevator doors from closing completely. Worse, the shoe was attached to a leg, and from what she could see through the four-inch opening, the leg was attached to a body.

She clapped a hand over her mouth to muffle an explosive hiccup as she heard a muttered groan from within the elevator. He wasn't dead, she realized. He might be injured, he might even be drunk, but at least he wasn't dead. Biting down on her lower lip, she gently prodded the white sneaker with the point of her umbrella. The foot jerked suddenly, and with a husky voice announced quite clearly, "No more autographs, ladies. I have a headache."

He was obviously a drunk, she thought. Not only that, but he was a drunk with an ego. Mercy punched the down button with her umbrella and the straining elevator doors slid open. For the first time she got a good look at the poor party animal sprawled on the floor— and what a party it must have been. His navy and white knit shirt was wrenched high above his waistband, revealing a wide expanse of smooth tanned skin. The collar of his shirt was stained with bright purple something-or-other, as was his neck, his jaw, and his chin. Purple drops sparkled throughout his matted dark gold hair and dripped off the tip of his nose. A blue baseball cap rested on the floor beside his head. The sight of that cap made her think of Tucker Healy, which brought forth yet another rib-jarring hiccup.

There were too many men in the world, Mercy thought irritably. When you started tripping over their bodies in elevators, something had to be done.

She ventured a step or two inside and knelt down, cautiously tugging on the hem of his jeans. "Hello? Are you all right? Can you hear me?"

"I don't wear Comfort Weave underwear," he said. "It itches."

Mercy stared at him, wondering if she had heard right. Then she tugged on his pants a little harder. "I'm not interested in your underwear, you idiot. I have problems of my own. You need to go home and sleep this off. You can't stay here."

He grunted and moved his head restlessly from side to side. His skin looked dry and tight, although a faint shimmer of perspiration glittered on his forehead. For the first time Mercy noticed that the air around him seemed to steam, and she gently touched a hand to his bare arm, feeling the heat there.

"I don't think you're drunk," she said.

His eyes opened suddenly and zeroed in on her. She'd never seen such a sparkling, luminous blue in all her life, an unsettling contrast to the waxy pallor of his skin. His dark lashes were tipped with gold, tangling with his matted, sweat-soaked bangs. "Drunk?" he repeated in a confused voice. "On one Icee?"

For the first time Mercy noticed the empty plastic cup in the corner. "What happened? Did you get mugged?"

He touched his purple chin. "I got slimed." His glittering eyes wandered to the neon-pink umbrella beneath her arm. "Ugly color."

The elevator bell sounded and the doors began to close. Mercy lifted her umbrella and punched the open button, then wedged the goose-head handle in the metal track to make sure the doors stayed open. She didn't want to be trapped in this tiny box with a sick egomaniac who very possibly had no underwear on. "Listen, you need some help," she said, getting to her feet. "I'm going to call a doctor. You just—"

"Hold on." He sat up ever-so-slowly, drawing up his knees and resting his sticky forehead in his hands. "Just . . . calm down. I saw a doctor today. He said I was sick."

"A medical wizard," Mercy muttered.

He stared at her through sticky fingers. "Said I should go home and rest, but . . . I'm having a little trouble getting there. Where am I?"

Mercy pushed her hat far back on her head and looked down at him apprehensively. "Chelsea Towers."

"I know *that*," he said. "What floor?"

"Fourth."

"*Fourth?*" He stared at her through his fingers. "Again? Damn elevator's running amok. Wouldn't get in it if I were you. You'll never get out again."

Mercy decided it was time to take control of the man, the damn elevator, and the situation. It wasn't her strong point—taking control—but she didn't see that she had a choice. Obviously he needed help getting to his apartment, and she doubted he could manage the stairs in his condition. She took a deep breath, measuring the elevator with round, dark eyes. She ought to be able to handle a short trip without going completely crazy. Probably. Maybe. Possibly.

She cleared her throat and squared her shoulders. "What floor do you live on?"

He started, as if he had forgotten she was there. "What? Oh. Top floor. Keep it to yourself. Need to protect my privates. *Privacy*," he corrected, knuckling his red-rimmed eyes with his fists.

Mercy stooped, freeing the umbrella handle from the door track. She took one last, longing look at the spacious, high-ceilinged hallway before reluctantly pressing the button for the eleventh floor. "Don't worry," she said hoarsely, trying to give herself a bit of reassurance as the doors slowly closed. "Everything's going to be just fine. It'll be over before you know it."

"Doctor said a couple of days at the most. Just a little virus."

Mercy threw him a withering glance. Her hands gripped the floppy brim of her hat, tugging it down over her ears to muffle the droning sound of the elevator. It couldn't last much longer. Just another few seconds . . .

She could have cried with relief by the time the doors finally opened on the eleventh floor. She grasped the blond man's hands and pulled him to his feet with a strength born of desperation. He swayed dizzily, and they both almost went down before Mercy regained her balance. "If you pass out," she hissed at him through clenched teeth, "I'll leave you in here to die, I swear to heaven I will."

"You'd make a great nurse." He leaned heavily against her, panting. "Wait a minute while I catch my breath. . . ."

"No." The walls were closing in on her, the ceiling pressing down. She hoisted his arm around her shoulders and lurched forward, nearly buckling under the weight of his six-foot frame. Just *walk*, will you?"

"You're really short," he said, squashing the crown of her hat with his chin.

"You're really sticky. It's a good thing I wore my rain slicker. I'll have to hose myself off when I get home." She dragged him across the threshold, exhibiting the awesome strength of a near-hysterical woman. Once in the hall-way, they staggered in place while Mercy sucked in fortifying breaths. "Oh, boy," she said with a gasp. "I should get a medal for this, I really should. All right, which way? Right or left?"

"Left," he said, and turned right.

Men were such pains. Mercy planted her rubber boots in the carpet and shook his arm. "What number? What's the number of your apartment?"

He took so long to answer, she was afraid he couldn't remember. "Eleven-C," he said thickly. "Down this hall. I can take it from here. Everything's under control now. Would you like my autograph?"

"Nothing would make me happier." Mercy groaned, urging him forward. "Here we go, one foot in front of the other. . . ."

Progress was slow. They took one step backward for every two steps forward, but Mercy managed to keep them both upright and moving in the right direction. She panted the hiccups right out of her—small consolation for the bruises on her poor toes. The man wasn't exactly light on his feet.

"Home sweet home," she said breathlessly, at long last reaching the white-paneled door at the end of the hall. She propped him against the wall, watching for a moment to make sure he would stay there. "All right? Good. Where's your key?"

"Oh . . . my key." He frowned, patting the pockets of his jeans with clumsy fingers. "I've got it here somewhere. . . ."

He pulled a tube of lip balm, a small bottle of aspirin, and a metal keyring from his pocket, then frowned as if trying to decide which of these might unlock the door. Exasperated, Mercy snatched up the keys. "I swear fate has it in for me," she muttered, trying one key after another in the lock. "The deli is closed now, so I won't get my cake. I really wanted that cake. I needed that cake." She found the right key and unlocked the door, pushing it open wide. "There you go," she said, turning back to the pale blond statue leaning against the wall. "You probably ought to take a couple of those aspirins and go straight to bed."

"You bet," he muttered, glassy-eyed and quite still.

"Don't lose this," she said, pressing the door key in his hand. "Look, are you going to be all right?"

"Just a little virus."

"Well . . . if you're sure."

"You bet," he said again, blinking once in slow motion. Suddenly his knees buckled, and he pitched forward, his chin catching Mercy hard in the middle of her forehead. She gasped with pain, staggering under the sudden weight. He hadn't passed out, thank goodness; Mercy wouldn't have stood a chance against nearly two hundred pounds of dead weight. He simply seemed to have lost the desire to remain vertical.

"Stand up," Mercy ordered, her face flattened against his chest. The heat from his fever practically sizzled the tip of her nose. "Here, turn around . . . we'll get you inside."

"Thought I'd never get here," he said hoarsely. He draped his arm across her shoulder, his hand cupping the curve of her breast

through the slicker. "I couldn't get away from
them . . . it's totally out of control . . ."

"Couldn't get away from who?" Mercy asked,
removing the hand.

"Those women. Audrey, Allison, Katie. Can't
remember the others. They were ruthless."

Mercy's lips twitched as she looked at his
grape-stained face. There was nothing like a
high fever to reveal a man's innermost fanta-
sies. Cleaned up, she had no doubt he would
be very attractive, but she didn't think he
would cause a stampede. "Another couple of
steps, Romeo. All right, hang on while I shut
the door. Good. Now which way to the bedroom?"

He rested his chin on the top of her head.
"You're really short."

"But I'm plucky." She hit a wall switch,
barely noticing the modernistic white-on-
white decor of the spacious living room, the
Deco chairs, and track lighting. "Which way?
Down the hall?"

"Down the hall," he acknowledged wearily.
He cursed as he stumbled over her toes yet
again. "Sorry. When I get a fever, I kind of lose
my equil . . . my equil . . . my balance. I'm
not usually this clumsy."

"Of course, you're not," Mercy replied, kicking the bedroom door open with her throbbing foot. She managed to flick the light
switch with her elbow. "I'm sure you're very
coordinated."

He nodded. "I am. I have medals. I had to

stop doing it though, cause my knees got bad."

Mercy would have laughed if she'd had the oxygen to spare. She had absolutely no idea what he was talking about, but, then, she doubted he did, either. She shuffled him over to the king-size bed in the center of the room, turned him around, and backed him up to the mattress. The bed was wide enough for three or even four, she noted with a tiny smirk, which was only fitting for a man who had won medals for his coordination.

"Down, boy," she said, putting her index finger on his chest and giving a tiny little push. He swayed on his feet for a moment, gave a world-weary sigh, and tumbled backward on the bed. Mercy grinned. The world would be a better place if all men were so easily manipulated. "Be good and rest while I fetch the aspirin for you. You dropped it in the hallway."

"I've had a very bad day," he mumbled, throwing his arms above his head. "I'm going to rest a minute, then I'll walk you home. . . ."

"What a good idea." Mercy realized she probably should have turned back the beautiful beige silk bedspread before he'd collapsed on it, but there was nothing she could do about that now. He was down, and she wasn't about to try and get him up again. She retrieved the aspirin from the hall, then found her way to the kitchen. It was decorated with a great deal of brass and flash, with see-through glass cabinets, Carrera marble counters, and modernistic fixtures. Everything looked perfectly coordinated, terribly expensive, and cold as ice. Mercy actually felt goosebumps rising on her skin while she filled a glass with water from a faucet shaped like a cobra rearing to strike. Her own apartment had been sub-leased from an old family friend who had gone on a three-month sabbatical to Europe, but the decor was nicely haphazard; a combination of warm colors and country prints that made her feel right at home. She much pre-ferred it to this futuristic wonderland.

Back in the bedroom, she saw that her patient had been busy. His shirt and jeans were on the floor, along with his sneakers. He'd thrown the bedspread off the bed, but he had pulled the sheet up to his waist. His eyes were closed.

"I have your aspirin," she whispered.

He frowned, turned his face into the pillow, and began to snore softly.

Mercy sat down on the edge of the bed, pulled off her hat, and took a long drink from the glass she held. Studying him, she couldn't help but notice one or two things. His chest, which was flushed with fever and glittering with perspiration, was beautifully molded with lean, rippling muscles. What she could see of his stomach looked rock-hard and flat as a board. Mercy's gaze traveled a little lower, to the outline of his narrow hips beneath the pale blue sheet. Mesmerized, she slowly raised the glass to her lips and drained the last of the water. She had a very bad habit of comparing every man she met with Tucker Healy, and they inevitably came up wanting. This man, however, didn't seem to want for anything— with the exception of a little soap and water.

Mercy didn't know what he had on beneath that sheet, but she knew for a fact it wasn't Comfort Weave underwear. For a brief moment she wondered about taking a little peek to see for herself, then sternly reprimanded herself for even considering such a thing. "You poor man," she whispered sympathetically, setting her glass on the bedside table. "Fallen gravely ill, and no one to care for you but a compulsive hiccuper who is too curious for her own good. Well, what to do now?" She put the back of her hand to his forehead and frowned. "You're terribly hot. If that fever doesn't come down soon, I'm calling a doctor."

His head twisted on the pillow and a low groan rumbled in his throat. Suddenly his eyes opened, he looked straight at Mercy, and smiled. It was an incredible smile for a man who was flat on his back and half out of his mind with fever. It was sweet and slow, tucking up the corners of his eyes and carving deep creases in his cheeks. "Hi," he said huskily.

Mercy stood up, eyeing him warily. His smile was a thing of beauty, but she didn't trust that excited light in his eyes. "Hi," she replied slowly. "How are you feeling?"

"Never better. Why are you dressed?" He lifted the sheet in a welcoming gesture. "Come back to bed."

"Oh, dear." Mercy had her answer now—yellow boxers with white piping. There wasn't a spare ounce of flesh on him, and heaven knew she could certainly see most of his flesh. "You're a little confused. I'm the one who found you in the elevator, remember? Why don't you cover up again? You shouldn't get chilled."

"Come and keep me warm." He plucked at her slicker with his fingers, but he couldn't get a grip.

"You're hot enough, believe me."

His blue eyes glittered up at her, and bright red spots burned high on his cheeks. "I want you next to me. Every sweet, soft inch of you."

Lordy, Lordy. He might be wandering in a dreamworld, but he made it sound like a lovely place to visit. Mercy watched in wide-eyed amazement as his fingers closed over her wrists. He drew her hand close to his face, his lips pressing against her palm in a gentle, tingling sucking motion. She felt a powerful lifting sensation in her chest, a purely sexual response to him as a man.

Drawing a sharp breath, she whipped her hand away. "I'm going to get a cold cloth for your forehead," she said breathlessly. "It might help cool you down a little. You . . . stay put."

"I smell grapes," he said. The expression of sleepy rapture suddenly vanished from his face. "Y'know what? I think I spilled the wine."

Mercy couldn't help but smile, though her nerve endings were still prickling like sparklers. There was something terribly appealing about the combination of helpless blue eyes, boyishly rumpled hair, and a Chippendales dancer's body. "No way. Not a coordinated guy like yourself."

He nodded. "I've got medals." He turned over on his side tugging up the sheet until it covered his shoulders. "I don't feel so good. Maybe I'm coming down with something. . . ."

He sighed and closed his eyes once more, his fingers curled next to his cheek. He looked like an exhausted child. His lips were parted in a sulky curve that hinted at restlessness, but his breathing seemed deep and even. Mercy thought he might sleep for a while. She shrugged out of her heavy rain slicker and tossed it over a Deco chair near the gas fireplace, then went to the bathroom and soaked a heavy velour washcloth in cold water. When she returned, her patient was wandering around his bedroom, the blue sheet wrapped around his middle like a toga.

"Can't find my shoes," he said hoarsely, shaking his head as he gazed vaguely around the room. "I'll walk you home soon as I find my shoes." He fixed her with a curious, if somewhat glassy-eyed stare. "What's your name?"

"Mercy."

He thought about that for a second, then gave her a lopsided grin. Taking advantage of his distraction, Mercy took him by the hand and led him back to the bed. Immediately he collapsed on the mattress, curling up in a fetal position. "S'been a wonderful night," he mumbled.

"Hasn't it, though?" Mercy covered him with the bedspread and gently placed the damp cloth on his forehead. He seemed a little cooler, but still she hesitated to leave him, fearing he might decide to walk off his balcony in search of his shoes.

She looked at the rigid, uncompromising lines of the chair. She visualized herself sitting like a little soldier throughout the long night, babysitting a man whose name she didn't even know. Then she imagined meeting Tucker Healy the next morning, looking and feeling like one of the living dead. Tucker, of course, would radiate charm and vitality. His hair would shine, his eyes would dance, his smile would dazzle. He would be much prettier than she would be. It was a depressing prospect.

She kicked off her rubber boots, cursing her marshmallow heart.

Two

Mercy knew before she'd opened her eyes that she had done a very foolish thing. Her entire body was one convoluted cramp—her head was fused to one shoulder, the muscles in her neck were petrified, and her feet were bloodless and limp as sausages. It had been a grave mistake to sleep through the night in that torturous chair. Now she was paralyzed from the ears down.

She opened her eyes in painful, quarter-inch stages. She saw yellow rubber boots on the carpet. She saw a beige silk bedspread pooled nearby, and a blue sheet dangling off the end of the bed. And then she saw six feet of bronzed masculinity stretched out on his side on the mattress. His back was to Mercy, hazy morning sunlight tracing the bewitching hollows of bone and sinew. Her gaze followed the sweet line of sloping shoulders, tapered waist, and slightly rounded hip. His boxer shorts were riding low, revealing a pale stripe of baby-smooth skin below the small of his back.

An unfamiliar stillness settled inside her as she watched him with a softly unfocused stare. She didn't think about the awkwardness of her situation. She didn't think at all. She simply drank in the sight of him, and for a suspended moment, the world and all its tiresome complications drifted far away. Her appreciation was elemental, almost primitive. His body was remarkably beautiful.

She wished she were someone else right now. Someone who could explore the sleepy excitement she was feeling, knowing that beginnings were still possible. Someone who could smile and luxuriate in the sensual awakening of female curiosity. Someone who had never met Tucker Healy.

Tucker. Mercy came fully awake in a split second, burying her face in her hands. How could she have forgotten? Like a tornado, he was due to touch down in her life any minute, turning everything upside down and inside out. And she wasn't ready. Emotionally, physically, mentally . . . she wasn't ready. She had been incredibly lonely the past few weeks, a stranger in a strange town, but there had been a quality of healing, as well. She wasn't prepared to have it all blow up in her face again. She knew darn well that Tucker would try to convince her to believe in him again. He would be playful and sweet, with a touch of vulnerability. He would swear to her that the other women meant nothing to him, which she imagined was probably true. And he would tell her that she was the only stable and constant influence in his life, which was also true.

And finally he would tell her he loved her, which would break her heart all over again, because in his own way, he did.

Wide-eyed, Mercy sat up a little straighter in the chair. She'd given all she had to give. She'd known it when she'd packed up and left New York two months earlier. It had been the coward's way out, but a way out, nonetheless. In the back of her mind, she had nourished a vague hope that once her self-esteem was healthy again, she would be capable of taking risks in a new relationship. But that would never happen as long as Tucker was in her life, making her feel guilty and not taking no for an answer.

There was no time to lose. She stood up, wincing and biting her lip as she moved stiffly about the room, picking up her hat, her coat, her boots. She would go back to her apartment, shower and change, and pack an overnight bag. And then, like the sadder but wiser woman she was, she would run away. A long weekend at a nice Motel 6 should do the trick, she thought. Tucker couldn't stay in Denver indefinitely. His telegram had said that he had pulled a muscle in his shoulder, giving him a temporary vacation from playing base-ball. She couldn't imagine he had much more than two or three days before he would be expected back again.

Two or three days playing hide-and-seek. She could manage that.

Before she left the room, she tiptoed over to the bed to check on her patient. He had his face buried in a pillow, but when she touched the smooth skin on his back, it felt cool. The fever was down. She stared at his sleep-tousled blond head for a moment, feeling a strange tenderness catch like a trapped breath in her throat. Not knowing why, she leaned over and brushed her lips lightly against his hair. "Take care," she whispered.

Naturally she bypassed the elevator, juggling her boots, coat, and hat in her arms as she hurried down seven flights of stairs. The metal treads were cold on her bare feet, and the air-conditioning was already blasting through the stairwell. She was shivering, huffing, and puffing by the time she opened the door to the fourth floor. And there she stopped dead, staring down the long hallway at the unmistakable figure lounging against her door.

Tucker. She held her breath to stifle a renegade hiccup. He looked as if he had been waiting there for some time. He was leaning against the door, head tipped back, a peeved expression on his face. He wore a brilliant canary-yellow shirt, which set off his dark coloring, pleated khaki slacks, and rich leather moccasins. He looked much more beautiful than she had ever looked first thing in the morning. Irresistible Tucker, all broad shoulders and long legs and simmering resentment. He didn't like to wait for *anything*.

Mercy slowly backed into the stairwell, gently, gently easing the door closed. What to do, what to do? She could hardly loiter in her rosebud pajamas until he got discouraged and left. It was still early, but soon people would be up and about.

She looked up and down the stairs, chewing on her fingernail. She had two choices. She could put on all her rain gear and go walking in the bright May sunshine for a couple of hours, or she could go back upstairs from whence she'd come and check on her afflicted neighbor. That would be the kindest thing to do, she thought. The compassionate thing to do.

She pressed her nose against the frosted-glass window in the door, hoping Tucker might have gone. The pressure on the door was enough to close it completely. The latch clicked. Hearing the sound, Tucker swiveled his dark head in her direction. He straightened slowly, then began walking toward the stairwell.

Mercy took off up the stairs at a dead run.

Sam was being very, very quiet.

He didn't want to aggravate his delicate condition. His head was excruciatingly tender, his muscles were aching, and his field of vision was a blur of shapes and colors. His fever was gone, and he knew he was on the mend, but he didn't have the energy to care. He would have a glass of juice and a cup of coffee, then go quietly back to bed. And he would do his best to forget the utter fool he had made of himself the night before.

He may have been delirious, but Sam remembered Mercy the Good Samaritan quite vividly. He couldn't say what color her hair was, since she had been wearing some kind of floppy something on her head, but he remembered enormous brown eyes and a ridiculously short nose, and that heart-shaped mouth that always seemed to have a funny, sassy comeback for him. She'd been kind enough to rescue him from the big nasty elevator and help him to his apartment, and what had he done in return? He'd babbled on about his wonderful coordination and the medals he had won. To top that off, he'd generously offered her his autograph. Yes sir, that must have been quite a thrill for her, having a lunatic invalid offer his autograph, especially since she'd given no sign of recognizing him. Last and definitely most embarrassing, he retained a vague memory of trying to pull her into bed with him.

He would have liked to apologize to her for his fevered ramblings and thank her for her patience, but she was gone. He couldn't blame her. Probably it hadn't been the most entertaining evening she had ever spent. Then again, she might have laughed herself silly all the way home.

Feeling sad, weak, and deprived—though he couldn't put his finger on what it was he had been deprived of—he pulled on his threadbare terry cloth "sick robe" and wandered into the kitchen. He never felt particularly welcome in his kitchen—or anywhere else in his apartment, for that matter. The stark furnishings and anemic color scheme always gave him the shivers, but he put up with it because the interior designer responsible had been greatly in demand and exorbitantly expensive; therefore, qualified. Sam had grown up in Touqerville, a sleepy bedroom town deep in Idaho's farming country. Nothing in his early years had persuaded him that he knew the first thing about sophisticated living. He left the trappings of his high-profile lifestyle to the professionals.

He filled the coffee maker and turned it on, then turned it off again when the perking noises threatened to split his skull in half. No coffee this morning. No toast either; he didn't have the energy to chew. Just a cold glass of orange juice and back to bed for him. And when he felt better, he would punch out good old Dr. Jack Menzies for daring to call this hellish affliction a "little virus."

He went to the refrigerator with glass in hand, poured himself some juice, then quietly shut the door. "Because a day without orange juice," he intoned in a gloomy voice, "is like a day without sunshine. We can't have that, can we, Sammy?"

As he turned around, a woman walked

through the doorway. They gasped in startled unison; the glass of juice hit the floor with an earsplitting crash.

Her gasp rose to a shriek. "Aaaaggh!"

Sam staggered backward, eyes closed, hands over his ears. He didn't care if this person had snuck into his apartment to murder him. He just wanted her to be quiet while she did it. "Don't scream. I can't take it. Just . . . don't."

A pause, then a tiny whisper: "Sorry. I didn't expect you to be in here."

"I didn't expect you, either." Sam opened one eye, squinting at her, then the other, as recognition dawned. Minus the hat and rain slicker, Mercy the Good Samaritan was an adorable half-pint of femininity—five feet two at the most, with long dark hair and wispy bangs framing startled doe-eyes. And if he wasn't mistaken, she was wearing pajamas. The bottom half fit nicely. The top half strained heroically over her full, unfettered breasts. "Mercy," he said, and meant it.

"You remembered my name." Mercy stared at him intently, trying to decide if he was lucid or not. All in all, he looked much better than he had the night before. Grape had not been his color. "How are you feeling?"

"Better," he said quite honestly. He wasn't feeling deprived any longer. His memory had not done justice to his Good Samaritan. With her generous, too-good-to-be-true lips and those Alice-in-Wonderland eyes, she was a fascinating combination of sweet and sexy, sprite and temptress. The pajamas belonged to a Girl Scout, the body beneath to a fallen angel. She stood still, hands clasped before her, yet she possessed an unmistakable vitality that projected through the room like a sun-shower. For the first time in nearly a year, Sam's kitchen actually felt warm and cozy. Softly he said, "I'm glad you came back."

Something in the tone of his voice made Mercy feel a little shaky. Not scared-shaky, but pleasantly unstable. "I was worried about you last night. You seemed so . . ."

Tucker, she thought suddenly, her mouth dropping open in midsentence. What was the matter with her? She'd completely spaced-out again. He'd been fast on her heels up seven flights of stairs—and Tucker was famous for his speed. She didn't think he'd actually gotten a good look at her, but she wasn't certain. And any minute now, he could—

The doorbell suddenly rang, then someone knocked, then the doorbell rang again.

"Impatient little bugger," Sam said, frowning. He knew he didn't have any appointments or interviews scheduled, and his friends knew better than to show up on a Saturday morning before noon.

Mercy nodded miserably. "That he is."

Sam stared at her. He didn't like what he was feeling. It had something to do with the way she said "*he*," as if their visitor were some sort of local Colorado deity. "You know this person pounding on my door?"

She shifted her weight onto her other foot,

looped her hair behind her ears, and bit down on her lower lip, all at once. "Oh . . . I think I might."

"Who might he be?"

"He might be Tucker Healy, my ex-fiancé. And it might be a good idea if we don't answer the door."

Sam's headache was coming back in full-force, but he didn't think it was due to his little virus. "How does he know you're here?"

"He doesn't," Mercy said quickly. "He's . . . following a hunch. I was on my way back to my apartment and—"

"You live here?"

"Down on the fourth floor. I was on my way back this morning, and—"

"You stayed here all night?" Sam visualized her Bambi brown eyes watching over him anxiously throughout the night. Yes, he liked that.

"Your fever was so high, I was afraid to leave you." Mercy jumped and flushed as the doorbell rang again, her hands tugging distractedly through her hair. "Why doesn't he go away? Where was I? Oh, when I went back downstairs, I saw Tucker—my ex-fiancé—waiting for me. I ducked back in the stairwell, but I think he must have heard the door close. When I ran back up here, he followed me."

"Why?"

"Because he wants to see me."

"No," Sam said impatiently, "why are you hiding from him?"

"I don't wish to see *him*." Trying to change

the subject, she added quickly, "Why don't I clean up this mess on the floor? We both have bare feet, and you really don't need any more pain in your life this morning."

"I'll clean up later. Just watch your step." Sam stared at her grimly as the knocking started up again. Her eyes were enormous, the cadence of her breathing breaking into quick catches. "Do I answer the door or hide under my bed?"

"He'll go away," Mercy muttered, getting down on her knees and gingerly picking up pieces of glass. "Eventually."

Sam didn't like this persistent Tucker Healy person who was making all kinds of racket and aggravating his aching head. He'd never met him, but he knew with absolute certainty that he didn't like him. "Is he violent?"

Mercy kept her head bent. "No. Just spoiled."

He wasn't *the only one*, Sam thought, watching the hazy sunlight pick out the dark gold highlights in her hair. There was a sexy, delectable woman on his kitchen floor, and the wild flush of excitement on her face didn't have a damn thing to do with him. How humbling. How irritating. "Why don't you want to see this nonviolent, spoiled person?"

"It's a long story." Mercy sat back on her heels, listening. "I think he's gone. I don't hear anything." She moved to stand up, one hand on the floor for balance, the other open and cradling several large pieces of glass. Then her bare feet suddenly slipped on the sticky floor, going right out from under her. She came down hard on her bottom, and the hand holding the glass closed instinctively. Immediately she felt the jagged edges cut into her palm, sending a hot wave of pain shooting up her arm. "*Ouch!* Hells bells, that hurt . . ."

"Here, let me see." Sam was beside her instantly, helping her to her feet. "It's all right, let me help."

Breathless and light-headed, Mercy shook shards of glass and a spray of blood from her hand. "I think I need a little bandage," she said faintly.

"What an optimistic soul." Sam pushed her down into a chair, taking her hand gently in his. "This is going to need stitches."

"It's not that bad." Mercy doubled over, putting her head between her knees to battle the nausea and dizziness. She focused hazily on the droplets of blood dripping from her hand to the floor. "I'm making a mess here. If you'll hand me a couple of paper towels, I'll wipe this up."

"A clean floor is certainly first on *my* priority list," Sam muttered. He went to the sink and rinsed a clean dish towel under cold water, then knelt down by Mercy and wrapped it tightly around her hand to stem the bleeding. Her eyes stared at him blankly, prompting him to click his fingers in front of her nose. "Hello there? Are you going to pass out on me?"

While she thought about it, another wave of

nausea assailed her. "No. I'm just feeling light-headed." She tried to smile. "Sorry. I've had this problem ever since I was little. I see blood, I see stars. It's kind of like Tucker and hiccups."

He had no idea what she was talking about, but simply hearing the name Tucker again irritated him. Still, first things first. "Sit tight," he said. "I'll be right back."

Mercy watched him with limpid eyes as he went to the telephone on the wall and made a brief call. She couldn't hear what he was saying over the ringing in her ears. What a pair, she thought woozily. The sick and the afflicted.

"He's on his way," Sam said, pulling up a chair beside her.

Mercy cradled her hand in her lap, feeling the steady throbbing radiate through her body like heat shimmers. "Who?"

"The doctor."

"Doctors don't make house calls."

"Mine does. It won't take long, he just lives down the street."

The silence stretched and grew. Mercy slid her gaze sideways, like a schoolgirl sneaking looks at the boy in the next seat. In profile, his face was . . . well, riveting was the only word that came to her hazy mind. The lazy twist of his lips, the chiseled jaw and the deep-set, shaded eyes reflected a stark sensuality. His was not a handsome face in the classic tradition, but definitely unforgettable. And somehow strangely familiar.

"I don't know your name," she said suddenly.

"Sam. Just . . . Sam." He couldn't remember the last time he'd been just Sam. It felt nice, like meeting an old friend again.

"Good-neighbor Sam." She smiled faintly. "I'm Mercy Sullivan, and I want you to know this is a great treat for me."

Sam looked at her warily. The last thing in the world he wanted was for her to recognize him. It was so seldom The Rebel Without a Pause was able to pause and be himself. "Why?"

"Here I am sitting next to a man who has won medals for his coordination. This must be my lucky day."

She was teasing him. Sam let out a breath he hadn't been aware he was holding. "You can't hold me responsible for anything I said last night. I was blabbering."

"Oh." She lowered her gaze humbly. "I guess that means you won't be taking me home to meet your mother?"

He threw her a startled look, then began to laugh weakly. "Mercy," he said, holding his aching head in both hands.

"What?"

"Nothing. Just Mercy."

"Overreacted a little, don't you think, Sam?" Jack Menzies asked sardonically. "She didn't need a single stitch, just a butterfly bandage.

All that malarky about severed arteries . . . you should be ashamed of yourself."

"It looked like a lot of blood for such a small person to lose," Sam said defensively. "Besides, how else was I supposed to get you over here? You don't make house calls."

Jack looked across the living room at the pajama-clad figure standing in front of the long windows. "You could have been honest. You could have said you had an injured woman here who was extremely cute and wearing her jammies."

Sam followed the direction of Jack's gaze. Mercy was rocking up and down on her bare toes, her expression pensive as she stared at the street below. Dusty sunlight wreathed her shining hair, giving her an unearthly glow. "Would you have come?"

The good doctor smiled sweetly. He was a fair-haired man in his late thirties with sparkling gray eyes and a smooth baby-face that women adored. "You've been my best friend for years, Sam. How could you even ask that question?"

"Go home, Jack," Sam said, opening the door.

"She's not your usual type, you know. Why is she wearing pajamas? A negligee I could understand."

"Good-bye, Jack."

"Do you know what else I noticed? She isn't drooling over you. What a novelty. I like this girl, Sammy—she's unimpressed by you. Maybe there is justice in the world, after all."

Sam helped his friend out the door with a firm hand on his back. "Nice seeing you, Jack. Don't get hit by a bus on the way home."

"We'll have to have a long talk someday," Jack called over his shoulder to Mercy. "I think you're a very discerning person. I could tell the minute I set eyes on you that you weren't one of those women who went weak at the knees because of a silly underwear—"

Sam shut the door on his friend and turned to smile at Mercy. "What a guy."

A smile hovered on her lips. "What was that about silly underwear?"

"Jack's never been quite right since medical school. Sniffed too much formaldehyde, or something." Sam stuck his hands in the pockets of his robe and tried to look very sad. "A pancake short of a stack, I'm afraid. Still, he knows his business, and he loves making house calls."

Her smile grew. "He was very nice. Strange, but nice."

"Which just about describes all my friends." Sam was feeling much better. Much better, he thought, looking at the warm light that detailed the tender roundness of her breasts. Pajamas were much underrated, particularly when backlit by a windowful of sun. "Would you like coffee?" he asked dreamily. "Some nice hot coffee? You wouldn't have to move a muscle. I could bring it in here to you."

Mercy shook her head and squared her shoulders. "No, I should go and let you get your rest. I shouldn't have imposed in the first place. Hopefully Tucker's gone—*hic*—by now. He's not a patient person."

Tucker. There was that name again, and once again Sam experienced the same prickling antagonism. "Maybe you ought to stick around a while longer, to be sure."

"Thank you, but no." She scooped up her rain gear from a nearby chair, trying to hold it all without using her injured hand. "I shouldn't have panicked the way I did when I saw—*hic*—him. It was childish. I'm sorry I bothered you. Oops, I dropped a boot."

"He gives you the hiccups?" Sam asked, a curious inflection in his voice. He picked up the boot and trailed after her to the door, watching her hips sway with an enthralling rhythm that was marred by an occasional ferocious hiccup. "What is it, an allergic reaction or something?"

"The doctor said I would outgrow it," Mercy muttered. "That was—*hic*—ten years ago."

"How did you expect to marry the guy? You'd hiccup yourself to death."

"It doesn't happen all the time, only when I'm anxious or upset or feeling highly emotional."

Sam couldn't remember ever having that effect on a woman. He'd certainly made them highly emotional, but he'd never made a woman hiccup.

"Hold your breath," he said abruptly. He wanted those hiccups stopped and he wanted them stopped now.

"Doesn't work. I'd just pass out and keep on

hiccuping. Could you get the door? My—*hic*—hands are full."

Sam opened the door, staring down at her. "How about a glass of water?"

"Never works."

He scowled, tucking the boot between her chin and the wadded-up raincoat. "What *does* work?"

"Oh, sooner or later I'll get distracted and start thinking about something else besides Tucker—*hic*—and they'll go away." She smiled at him, her eyes bright with introspective humor. "And sooner or later they'll come back again, and there's nothing anyone can do about it. It's inevitable."

"Inevitable," Sam repeated softly. "You know, I really hate that word."

And then he kissed her.

He bent his head and closed his lips deliberately over hers, taking a long and unforgettable drink. He went into it using all the experience and expertise that he had gathered in ten years of enthusiastically requited flirtations. Three seconds later he was melting in a seizure of need that was more powerful than anything he had ever known. One kiss, yet his hips were stirring and his mind was spinning and every part of him stung with the pressure to know more of her. Technique was abandoned. Thought evaporated. He remembered what it was like to lose himself, to wander blind and hot and sweet within someone else. He didn't worry about meeting expectations, or living up to a fantasy. As their tongues touched for the first time, a moan of pure pleasure came from deep within his throat.

Mercy jumped right in as if she'd been kissing him all her life. She didn't mean to, certainly hadn't planned to, but logic had deserted her with the first touch of his lips on hers. She forgot about the coat and boots and hat crushed between them, forgot about Tucker haunting the apartment building. There was only Sam, the feel of him and the brand-new taste of him; the incredible satin smoothness of his lips and the liquid fire of his tongue. She stood on tiptoe, straining and gasping and awash in sensations. She hadn't expected anything like this, and the shock added to the currents of pleasure shivering through her. She didn't even know him, she thought dazedly. She didn't even know him. . . .

When he finally lifted his head, her eyes were wider and darker than he had ever seen them. Her lips were wet and swollen, her skin flushed with luminous heat. She looked shell-shocked, sexy, and adorable. Looking down at her, desire rocked through him like thunder after lightning.

"Oh, boy," she whispered hoarsely.

Again, Sam thought hungrily, his head dipping toward her, his eyes drifting closed. But sanity was returning, and he pulled back at the last second, his breath coming in hard, painful catches. He'd scare her to death if he kept this up. Hell, he would scare himself to death.

"I hope that helped," he said raggedly, deliberately taking one step back from temptation.

Mercy's gaze was caught helplessly in his. "What?"

"Your hiccups. I thought we'd try to—" He paused, taking in a shaky breath. "I thought we'd try and scare them out of you."

"Scare them," Mercy echoed huskily. She still couldn't quite believe what had happened, or her own response to it. She felt as if she'd been scorched.

"Don't thank me." A satisfied smile shaped his lips as he realized his impulsive and unorthodox treatment had worked. She was no longer hiccuping. He wasn't even sure she was breathing. "I'm happy to help out."

"I think I should go home now," she whispered, more to herself than to him. She walked past him into the hall, the sleeve of her rain slicker dragging on the carpet behind her.

Three

Tucker had abandoned his post in front of Mercy's apartment, but he'd left an empty candy wrapper beneath the door bearing a typically Tucker message.

You can run but you can't hide, Cookie. Staying at Sheraton till Sunday—would rather stay with you.

"Cookie," Mercy muttered, kicking the door closed behind her. She hated that nickname. Tucker had gifted her with it when she'd been a round and rosy thirteen-year-old with a passion for Oreos. She'd hated it then and she hated it now. One day she would work up the courage to tell him so.

She sat down on the sofa and tried to settle on a mature way to handle the sticky situation she was in. Instead, her mind took an abrupt U-turn back to Sam and his surefire cure for hiccups. Her lips twitched and her toes curled in the thick carpet as she relived The Kiss—so unexpected, a stunning glimpse of sensual promise. What a strange, appealing, unpredictable man. She wasn't at all offended that he had kissed her; she thought of it as a delightful compliment. She was also surprised and gratified at her own enthusiastic response. It was very encouraging. Her breakup with Tucker had obviously been healthy for her. She had a funny feeling inside, like a breath of sweet, cool air had whispered through her, waking her up, nudging her toward full-blown emancipation. All she needed was time to continue her metamorphosis from a clinging caterpillar to a dancing butterfly. She had come so far. She realized the mature thing would be to avoid Tucker at all costs—run from him, hide from him, duck him and ditch him. Healthy Cowardice—her new motto.

She spent the entire day at the Denver zoo. She spent the night at a Howard Johnson. On Sunday morning she snuck home for a change of clothes, darting from pillar to post in the lobby like a cat burglar, racing up the stairwell, and bounding into her apartment with the speed of light. The telephone was ringing as she got in; she gently placed a pillow over the offending instrument.

It was Tucker's last day in town, and she knew him well enough to realize he would stop at nothing to see her. Tucker had a lifelong habit of getting whatever he wanted, and this little game of hide-and-seek she had been playing would not amuse him. Again, Mercy saw the wisdom of Healthy Cowardice. She showered and changed to jeans and a tie-dyed T-shirt, slipped on a worn denim jacket, and tied her hair in a ponytail. The ponytail she stuffed into a navy-blue baseball cap, tugged low on her forehead. A pair of mirrored aviator sunglasses that covered half her face completed her unconventional outfit. Tucker would have to look very closely before he recognized this tomboy urchin as his once-devoted fiancée. He liked women to look like women, with hips and breasts displayed in figure-hugging dresses, with cherry-red lips and long, flowing hair. Mercy had always obliged in the past, but no more. As she studied herself in the mirror, she was aware of a feeling rising like a tide from the toes of her comfortably worn sneakers to the roots of her hair. She tried to identify it, but it wasn't until she was skipping back down the stair-well that she finally began to understand.

She felt perfectly, wonderfully natural—Mercy Rose Sullivan through and through. What a splendid, glorious thing it was finally to please herself. The imposter Cookie was no more. Long live Mercy Rose—the rebel.

By Sunday morning Sam Christie felt like a new man—strong as a horse and twice as hungry. He ate toaster waffles and microwave sausages and drank a quart of orange juice, then spiffed himself up nicely in khaki twill slacks and a black Hermès knit shirt. It was time to go visiting, to thank his lovely neighbor with the adorable pink jammies for her TLC on his behalf. Mercy. Sam had dreamed about her throughout the night, quite the most stimulating dreams he had had since high school, when a cheerleader named Tracy Grace Parsons had inspired his subconscious to startlingly imaginative heights. Of course, he had never had the courage to speak more than two words to haughty Tracy Grace, and she had brought him nothing but acne and angst. Mercy Sullivan was something else altogether, gently approachable, quite funny, startlingly frank, and intensely beautiful in a pure, completely unselfconscious way. After so many years of living as the prey of the blood-sucking media, so many years of being pointed at and fawned over and flattered, Sam was utterly charmed by her sincerity and casual friendliness. Ambition, greed, pettiness—he could sniff them in the air, but Mercy was as fresh and natural as a breath of spring. The kiss they had shared had affected him as if he'd never kissed before. He knew with a bright, profound certainty that he was standing on the threshold of something extraordinary.

Damn, but he was glad he'd passed out in the elevator.

He splashed on some Obsession cologne for a finishing touch, then washed most of it off again with soap and water because he didn't want to seem as if he were trying to impress her. Besides, he had hopes of taking her on a nice long drive in the mountains, and a little Obsession went a long way in a closed car.

He had his hand on the knob when someone knocked on the other side of the door. His mind was on Mercy. His first optimistic thought was that she might have dropped by to check on him, and he opened the door without checking through the peephole. It was a mistake.

"Colin Bloodworth, *World Weekly*." A short, reed-thin fellow with a bobbing face and a wispy Vandyke beard stuck out his hand. He wore a thin-lipped look of ambition Sam recognized only too well. "I'd like to ask you a few questions, Mr. Christie. You were spotted driving while intoxicated on Friday evening. An eyewitness also claims you nearly ran a pedestrian down in front of The Circle K convenience store. Have you any comment?"

"Nothing you could print."

The reporter blocked Sam's effort to shut the door with one brown saddle shoe. "It would probably be better for you to present your side, Mr. Christie. Otherwise our readers may receive a rather inaccurate impression of the incident."

"There was no incident," Sam said tightly, "and an inaccurate impression would be a hell of an improvement over the bald-faced lies you usually print in that rag of yours. Now move your foot, or I might lose my temper."

"Are you threatening a respected member of the press, sir?"

"Not at all. I'm threatening you." Sam's fingers curled into fists at his sides. "Clearly and simply, so you will have a very accurate impression of my intentions."

Colin moved his foot back an inch or two, but not quite enough for Sam to close the door. "I'm not the only one who got wind of this incident, Mr. Christie. There are representatives of several newspapers waiting in the lobby, as well as reporters and camera crews from local television stations. I was able to slip past the security guards—you can be sure they'll do the same sooner or later. You have no choice but to face the consequences of your behavior."

"You sound like my third-grade teacher," Sam said with deceptive mildness. Then, without warning, he swung the door wide and grabbed the obnoxious reporter by his green bow tie. "I don't like you, Mister. I've met reporters I didn't care for, but I really, *really* don't like you. You've ruined a perfectly good day for me, and that's very irritating. I would like to do you bodily harm, but I won't because I'm a civilized man and I don't want bloodstains on my carpet."

He released the man with the same abrupt gesture one would use to shake off a leech, then kicked the door closed and locked it. Sam had been through this kind of thing several times in the past, when some innocent remark or act of his had been blown completely out of proportion. He would talk to his publicist on Monday morning and issue a statement, but in the meantime, he'd have to postpone his wishful plans for a Sunday drive with Mercy. The last thing he wanted was to draw attention to her. Besides, she had no idea who he was, and he wanted to keep it that way for as long as possible. Intuition told him that "Just Sam" would have a far better chance of impressing Mercy Sullivan than "The Rebel Without a Pause."

And, as that irritating little bugger Bloodworth had pointed out, sooner or later the reporters would find their way to his door. Either he escaped now, or he spent the rest of the day barricaded inside with his hands over his ears.

Sam made his decision quickly. He changed into ragged jeans bleached to almost white, a faded chambray shirt, and a soft leather vest. Cowboy boots added two inches to his height, and a battered Stetson completely covered his trademark Robert Redford hair. He slipped on a pair of sunglasses, then took them off again long enough to check the peephole for possible peepers. The coast was clear. Sunglasses in place again, hat tugged low on his forehead, he ran across the hall and ducked into the stairwell. The Rebel Without a Pause was on the move.

Mercy moved cautiously through the rows of cars toward her Volkswagen Rabbit, dodging and ducking whenever someone came or went in the underground parking lot. She knew she was being overly dramatic, but she had discovered she quite liked playing catch-me-if-you-can. One more day, and Tucker would be winging his way back to rejoin his team where he belonged, and she would be safely out of temptation's path. Until then, she was taking no chances.

Her car was parked next to a black Jeep Renegade. Keeping low, she tiptoed past the Jeep, head bent as she rummaged through her purse for her keys. When a dark Mercedes cruised past, she dove between the two cars with a giggle and a gasp. She didn't see the tall cowboy unlocking the door of the Jeep until she bounced off his back.

"Excuse me," she muttered, straightening her sunglasses and adjusting her baseball cap. "I'm terribly sorry."

"Don't worry about it." He barely glanced at her, the brim of his hat shading the entire top half of his face.

"I was just . . . walking to my car. I must have . . . tripped."

"No problem." He turned away from her, opening the door of the Jeep. "Have a good day."

"You, too." Mercy turned on her heel, then paused. There was something about his voice . . .

She looked over her shoulder to find him looking over his. She ducked her chin and slid her sunglasses to the tip of her nose; he did the same.

"Mercy?"

"Sam?"

Sam quickly tugged off his hat and glasses, feeling more than a little foolish in his western-style garb. "I'm sorry . . . I didn't recognize you. You look . . . different."

Mercy crinkled her nose, and her smile dawned. "I'm keeping a low profile. Tucker— you remember Tucker?—well, he doesn't leave town until tonight, so I'm hiding behind sunglasses and baseball hats till then." She paused, head tilted slightly to the side. "If I didn't know better, I'd think you were hiding from someone yourself. That's kind of a different look for you, isn't it?"

"No, no . . . I dress like this all the time," Sam muttered, his face turning beet red. Better that she think him a country bumpkin with a John Wayne complex than discover the truth. "I grew up on a potato farm," he added, as if that explained everything.

"A potato farm," Mercy repeated, looking vaguely confused.

Sam nodded, rocking up and down on the heels of his boots. It was time to change the subject. Fate had just presented him with a very nice present to make amends for Colin Bloodworth, and he intended to make the most of it. "So where do you go when you're keeping a low profile?"

"I haven't decided yet," she said thoughtfully. She put on her shiny aviator glasses once again, balancing them on the bridge of her absurdly tiny nose. "Somewhere where there is absolutely no chance of running into

Tucker. Maybe I'll tour the local water-treatment plant."

Sam glanced over his shoulder as a white station wagon with the Channel Five insignia painted on the side pulled up to the freight elevator. Two men got out and began unloading equipment. As casually as possible, Sam replaced his hat and glasses. "You should be able to come up with something a little more exciting than that."

"What? I didn't hear you. Why are you whispering?"

"I'm not whispering." Sam cleared his throat, glancing nervously at the camera crew. "I haven't quite managed to shake this sore throat of mine. Listen . . . I was going to take a drive up Rock Creek Canyon, go four-wheeling for a couple of hours. If your heart isn't set on going to the water-treatment plant, how would you like to come along?"

"I've never been four-wheeling," Mercy said. By now she had noticed the camera crew as well, and she frowned at them thoughtfully. "Look at that. I wonder what's going on."

"I couldn't say. If you've never been four-wheeling, you shouldn't pass up this opportunity." Careful to keep his face turned away from the reporters, Sam walked around the Jeep and opened the passenger door. "I promise you more thrills and chills than a trip to Disneyland. Besides, it will give us a chance to talk. I'd like to . . . talk . . . to you."

Mercy stared at him, wishing she could see his eyes behind his glasses. She wasn't quite sure what he had in mind when he talked about thrills and chills, but as an alternative to a water-treatment plant, what woman in her right mind would refuse? Besides, she wanted to spend the day with him. It was as simple as that. There was an idyll trembling like music in the air, and she couldn't resist it.

There was also the possibility he would kiss her again. That couldn't be overlooked. A beautiful spring day. Thrills and chills. The luscious anything-could-happen feeling that made her flesh prickle. Oh, it was so much more rewarding being a butterfly than a cat-erpillar.

With her fingers crossed behind her back for luck, Mercy climbed into the car. By the time he had walked around to the driver's side, she'd freed her hair and tossed her glasses in the backseat.

"I kind of liked you in that hat," Sam said.

She twisted her hair in a topknot, then grabbed the hat and plopped it back on her head, batting her lashes beneath a forehead full of tangled bangs. "I kind of liked it myself, actually. Tucker always thought my hair looked best when it was—"

Sam gently clamped his hand over her mouth. He was in a great hurry to escape this hotbed of overeager reporters, but he had to make an important point first. "I really don't like that name—Tucker. When I hear that name, it makes my teeth hurt. If I kept a cockroach for a pet, I would not name it

Tucker because a cockroach deserves better. What are the chances of getting through the rest of this day without hearing the *T* word?"

Mercy waited patiently until he removed his hand. "You're right. I apologize. I have been liberated physically, but mentally I may still have a few hang-ups. I will guard my tongue. *En avant.*"

Sam grinned at her slowly, totally charmed by the picture she made with her baseball cap perched crookedly on her head and her bangs in her eyes and wisps of dark-chocolate hair straggling about her neck. She was very much a woman, a fact somehow emphasized by her boyish clothes. And he, Sam Christie, the most fortunate man in the Mile-High City, had the entire day just to *appreciate* her. It was Christmas, it was his birthday, it was the Fourth of July, all rolled into one.

Damn, but he was glad he'd passed out in that elevator.

The day was sunny and the mountains had never been more beautiful. The aspen trees were heavily crowned with bright green leaves, the evergreens were thick and shaggy, and the stream beds were swollen with a healthy spring runoff. The road cutting deep into Rock Creek Canyon was narrow and indecisive, constantly snaking in and around and back on itself, revealing glimpses of shadowed meadows, granite cliffs, and monster waterfalls splashing over jagged white rocks.

The road could also have used a good resurfacing, thanks to the extreme weather changes that had created an obstacle course of dips, bumps, and potholes. "So this is four-wheeling," Mercy said, clutching the edge of her seat as Sam whipped the Jeep around yet another narrow S-curve. "I don't know why. We haven't had all four wheels on the ground yet."

"This isn't four-wheeling, you silly, beautiful woman." Sam took a hard right to avoid a major sinkhole in the asphalt. "This is a lovely Sunday drive."

They bounced over a rut in the road, Mercy squashing her cap on her head to keep it in place. "Is four-wheeling worse than this?"

"You don't mean worse," he corrected her kindly, his hair tumbled and snarled from the open window, his laughing eyes the color of the spring sky. He'd lost the cowboy hat and the sunglasses the second they'd left the city limits. "You mean better, more exciting, more challenging. Isn't that what you mean?"

Mercy buckled her seat belt. She couldn't imagine why she hadn't done it sooner. "I suppose that was what I meant."

"Of course it was." Sam suddenly slammed on the brakes, sending the Jeep skidding in a half circle in the middle of the road. "Almost missed the turnoff," he said. "It's a little hard to spot if you're not familiar with the area."

"What turnoff?" Mercy's eyes were wide and growing wider by the second. As far as she could see, they were driving straight off the paved road and into a thick forest of solid green. "There is no road here, Sam. There is *no road*. Where are you going?"

"On this road."

"You're trying to tell me you see a road?"

"Not exactly." He took his hand off the gear-shift long enough to rake the hair out of his eyes. "Some men would look at all these rocks and trees and see only obstacles. Do you know what I see when I look at these rocks and trees?"

Apprehensively she asked, "What?"

"Challenges."

"Oh, dear."

Mercy didn't speak again for the next thirty minutes. She made quite a lot of noise—squeaks, screams, squeals, and gasps—but she didn't actually speak. She was a gently bred young woman from upstate New York, accustomed to nice straight roads, smooth curbs, and a center passing-lane. Civilized driving. She had never traveled in a car that chewed up rocks and spit them out, a car that could climb straight up one side of a pine tree and down the other, a car that plowed fear-lessly through bubbling streams. She had never driven with a man who laughed like a pirate whenever they came upon a granite boulder or a fallen log waiting to be con-quered. Sam had no regard for the laws of gravity. His Jeep had no regard for the laws of gravity. They worked together, man and ma-chine, doing what they damn well pleased against all odds. The man did deliver on his promises. Disneyland had never had the effect on her stomach that four-wheeling did. More than once, she stopped praying long enough to stare with amazement at the unshakable concentration in his face. Every ounce of his physical and emotional energy was focused on conquering this mountain, on achieving the goal he had set for himself. Man and nature were locked in a fierce, private battle—respected enemies—and he was winning. Something told her that Sam made a habit of winning, though not to achieve personal glory. He seemed to be a man who needed to dominate only himself, to exceed his own limitations. Mercy couldn't help but feel excluded, even a little envious. What would it be like to have such self-confidence, to be in such control? This was *life*, something she had watched happening to others while she filled her days and nights meeting everyone's expectations but her own. But no more. She finally had the freedom to become herself, and she intended to do just that . . . providing she survived this Sunday drive.

Eventually they broke through the wooded terrain, turning onto a narrow track scratched into the edge of the mountain. As far as Mercy was concerned, it was a "good news-bad news" joke—they were finally on something close to a road again, but on the passenger's side, the road was bordered by . . . absolutely nothing. If she stuck her head out the window—which she did only once—she could see down, down, down to a water-filled gorge. It looked like a ten-mile drop, but it was probably closer to seventy-five feet.

She pulled her cap over her eyes and slumped down in her seat with a whimper. There she stayed, stiff as a board, until the Jeep finally came to a halt. She tipped back her cap, opening one eye to peer at Sam. His back was resting against the door, one arm stretched casually across his seat.

"Was that fun," he asked, "or what?"

"I think it was fun," Mercy replied slowly. She sat up, relieved to discover they had stopped in a harmless meadow bordered by strands of tall cottonwood trees. The dirt track they had been following had widened to a gravel road, which was very comforting. "Where are we?"

"Almost at the bottom of the canyon," Sam said regretfully. "All the fun stuff is over. From here on the road is fairly tame."

Mercy stifled a sigh of relief. "Oh, well. All good things must come to an end. Do you do this four-wheeling thing often?"

"Actually, when I want to have some serious fun, I go to southern Utah to the sand dunes, or better yet, down to Baja. Or Alaska—Alaska has some backcountry trails you wouldn't believe."

She stared at him. "Serious fun? You mean, this wasn't serious fun?"

Sam grinned, waving his hand dismissively in the air. "Nah. This was mild amusement.

I'll let you know when we're having serious fun."

Alaska. Baja. Southern Utah. It occurred to Mercy that most men wouldn't be able to afford to spend so much time or energy on serious fun. "Sam? What is it you do for a living?"

Sam blinked, inwardly cursing himself for not guarding his tongue. He didn't want to lie to her, but neither was he ready to burst his bubble of anonymity. He'd found a new friend, a beautiful and desirable woman who was quite content to spend the day with "Just Sam." She accepted him at face value, with no preconceived notions or prejudices. He didn't want to give that up, not yet. "I'm in sales," he said. Which was true. He had endorsed a range of products from ski clothing to the infamous Comfort Weave underwear.

Mercy frowned, as if she couldn't quite picture him as a salesman. "What do you sell?"

He shrugged, avoiding her sparkling, trusting gaze. "Things. Running shoes. Cologne. Beer."

"Running shoes, cologne, and *beer*?"

It was time to distract his new friend, Sam thought. She was looking skeptical, and he couldn't blame her. It wasn't every salesman that represented such a unique variety of products. He pushed open his door and got out of the car, drinking in the sweet perfume of meadow grass and pine. It was a moment or two before he realized he was growing shorter.

His cowboy boots were slowly sinking into a slimy, pea-green bog.

"Mercy?"

"What?" She still sounded preoccupied with the salesman thing.

"Do you know why this clearing is so green?"

"Why?"

"Because it's a swamp. I'm up to my shins in slime."

Mercy ducked her head quickly out the window. She saw what neither of them had noticed before—the grass in the meadow was moving ever so slightly, undulating with a gentle current. There were sounds she hadn't noticed before, as well—frog sounds, trickling sounds. "Sam . . . look at the wheels of the Jeep. We're up to our axles in this muck. I thought you *knew* this trail."

"I do know this trail." Sam tried to pull his boot out of the swamp and the swamp sucked it back in again. "But spring runoff has been pretty heavy this year, and all that water has to go somewhere. I can't help it if this place turned into a mudhole when I wasn't looking."

Mercy started chewing on a corner of her wide mouth. "So what do we do? Can we drive out of here?"

"We can try." Sam dropped back in the driver's seat with a muffled *oomph*, pulling his feet free with a mighty tug. "Why did I wear these stupid boots? I hate these stupid boots."

"But . . . I thought you dressed like that all the time?"

"I don't want to talk about the way I dress," Sam muttered. "We have more important things to worry about now. Like whether or not you're still going to be speaking to me in five minutes."

Mercy looked at him suspiciously. "Why wouldn't I be speaking to you in five minutes?"

"This isn't going to sound very chivalrous." Sam took a deep breath, dropping his forehead on the steering wheel. "I want you to get out and push, Mercy."

"*What?*"

"The only way we're going to get out of here is by rocking the Jeep—putting it in first and giving it some gas, then letting in the clutch, rocking it back and forth until we get enough momentum to drive out."

Mercy began to have a very bad feeling. In her mind, the word "swamp" had always been associated with poisonous snakes and killer alligators and man-eating fish. Logic told her this was not a problem in the Rocky Mountains; still, she had a very bad feeling. "I'd rather be the one who drives the Jeep, thank you."

He lifted his head, a sweet, persuasive smile gently tucking the corners of his eyes. "It wouldn't work, Mercy. You have to know what you're doing, or you dig yourself in deeper. I'm afraid this is just . . . one of those things."

He waited. Mercy held his gaze long enough to realize he was completely serious. Muttering under her breath about thrills and chills, she rolled up her jeans to her knees, then opened the car door and gingerly stepped out. It wasn't bad at first—she was much lighter than Sam and didn't sink as quickly. She made it to the rear of the Jeep before the ooze started seeping into the tops of her sneakers.

She bent over, placing her palms flat on the dusty metal. "Say when."

Sam poked his head out the window. "When I give it gas, you push. When I let off on the gas, you stop pushing. We rock it like a cradle. Okay? On the count of three." He started the engine, staring at the top of her head in the rearview mirror. "One . . . two . . . push."

She pushed. The Jeep actually moved forward two or three inches, then settled back in the green slime. Sam gave it a little gas, and she pushed again. Slowly, steadily, the Jeep began to rock, back and forth, back and forth, until suddenly Sam tromped down on the accelerator and the Jeep roared out of the swampy bog with a mighty lunge, bouncing up and over a rotted log to dry ground.

Sam gave a shout of triumph, shaking one fist in the air. From somewhere behind the Jeep, he heard Mercy give a resounding shout of her own, but it sounded more traumatized than triumphant. Slowly, slowly, his gaze went to the rearview mirror . . . and he swore softly beneath his breath.

She was sitting on her rump in a muddy patch of knotted lilies. Her legs were tangled in stringy clumps of bulbs and stems. Her arms were flailing up and down, tiny fists splashing up a mossy storm. He could be mistaken, but it resembled a temper tantrum to him.

He got out and grimly surveyed the situation. They were only separated by ten yards or so, but it was a damn nasty ten yards.

"I'm coming," he called. He took off his boots, setting them side by side on the grassy knoll. He rolled up his jeans, then the sleeves of his shirt. "Be right there."

Mercy, who had been watching him, had subsided into stunned silence. What was wrong with this man? Why wasn't he plunging through the swamp to assist her? She watched him carefully take off his watch, and she slapped her hand to her forehead in amazement, leaving a grasshopper-green print. The blood vessel in her temple threatened to burst. "Are you sure you wouldn't like to run home and change into your swimsuit? I don't mind marinating here until you come back, I truly don't."

Sam gave her a sweet smile. "Patience, angel. I know exactly how to handle this situation."

Gently, cautiously he picked his way through the swampy ooze. When he got close enough to assist her, Mercy glowered at him and held out one dirty hand. Sam took it in his, but instead of pulling her to her feet, he gallantly kissed the tips of her fingers.

"Accept my apologies for this unpleasant incident," he said. And without warning, he threw himself facefirst into the marsh.

Mercy's mouth worked convulsively, her

eyes taking up half her face as she stared at his spread-eagled body. "You . . . you crazy person! What are you doing? Sam! Can you hear me? Sam?"

He sat up. Moss was hanging off his nose and chin, and a water lily dropped over one ear. "I know women," he said, shaking the water out of his hair and sitting back on his haunches. "They demand equality. It was easier to get slimed right along with you than to suffer the guilt of being dry and clean."

When she could finally speak, the words came out in short breathless gasps. "That was the . . . stupidest . . . most asinine . . . idiotic thing . . . I ever saw in my life."

He nodded. "But don't you feel better?"

"No," she said, but her lips twitched, and she felt a funny lifting sensation in her chest, as if someone were tickling her from inside.

His bright blue eyes coaxed her. "Just a little bit?"

Her smile grew. Suddenly she was buffeted by a sun-shower of delight, a spiritual high she had no reference point to explain. She started to chuckle, then the chuckles turned to laughter. She laughed until she thought she would be sick, until the sky was spinning and her side was aching and tears were streaming down her dirty face. And each time she got herself under control, she looked at Sam and the laughter would start all over again. He was desperately trying to decide between giving in to the humor of the situation and possibly offending her, or remaining suitably contrite, and the struggle was visible on his face.

"Is this serious fun?" she managed, gasping for air and giggling like an idiot.

Sam tried to stand, tripped on a root, and went down hard on all fours. "This is serious swamp."

Mercy made it to her feet first. She held out her hand, and after a brief moment of hesitation, Sam allowed her to help him up.

"That was very chivalrous of you," he said, wiping a mossy beard off his chin. "For a moment there I wondered if you wouldn't try to dump me back down on my rump again."

Her generous mouth tugged up at the corners. "How could I, after your sacrificial swan dive? You don't leave anything to chance, do you?"

Watching her, his eyes darkened with a new intensity. She was so precious to him, so endearing, standing there like a bedraggled Girl Scout on a camping trip gone wrong. The humor in her cinnamon eyes and the sunlight sparkling through her scattered curls made his pulse come hard in his throat. "Not this time," he said softly, lifting his hand to rub a finger gently under her chin. "Not this time, Mercy Sullivan."

Mercy's heart began to beat quickly, like a startled doe's. A leftover giggle suddenly, inexplicably turned into a hiccup. She held her breath, staring at Sam and losing her smile completely.

"What was that?" Sam demanded.

"Nothing."

"Did you hiccup? Did I make you hiccup?"

Cheeks burning, she shook her head, then hiccuped again.

"Ha!" Sam grinned and tossed back his hair, the buccaneer once again. "Take *that*, Tucker Healy!" Then he beckoned to her with a crooked finger.

"What?" Mercy asked in a husky little voice.

"C'mere."

"I'm all wet—"

"I know." He took a single long step forward, tangled weeds clinging to his boots like stubborn ivy. He grasped the back of her head with both hands, fingers threading through her hair as his mouth swooped over hers. His kiss was hard, wet, and hungry, penetrating her, making her gasp and sigh. It had been so long since he'd held her—over twenty-four hours, and thirty-four long years before that.

I want you to remember this, he thought. *Remember me, not him.* But it was too hard to say the words, so he tried with all his heart to make her feel them.

And Mercy . . . she opened to him like a flower to sun, craving what he offered. She arched her body toward his, rising on tiptoes, clasping her hands around his neck and holding on for dear life. The hardness of his muscles, the faint rocking motion of his hips set fire to her senses. It felt so good to her, so right. Nothing had ever felt so right.

Their lips parted with a frantic sucking

sound as Sam lifted his head. "Did I hurt you?"

"No . . . oh, no." A chill wind suddenly swept through the canyon, biting through her damp clothes, and she shivered.

"It's getting late," Sam said, trembling as hard as Mercy, but for different reasons. He stepped back, rubbing his hands up and down her arms. "I'll take you home."

"Sam . . ."

"What?"

"Nothing." Not thinking at all, she went into his arms once again and buried her face tight against his chest. "Just . . . Sam."

Four

Sam turned off the headlights on the Jeep as they pulled into the underground parking garage.

"Why are we driving in the dark?" Mercy asked curiously.

"It's not dark." Sam's eyes whipped from side to side as he searched for newshound types. "The security lamps give off plenty of light. Besides, I love a challenge. Driving without headlights through a parking garage is a challenge."

Mercy didn't even question this. She'd seen the man at work conquering the Rocky Mountains. What was a little parking garage after that? "At least it makes us less conspicuous. We look as if we've been mugged by the Creature From the Black Lagoon. Do you think we can make it upstairs without anyone seeing us?"

"I hope so," Sam said with great feeling.

Naturally they used the stairwell. Mercy explained that she was terrified of closed-in places, that even driving in a car she had to have a window open, that she'd been this way ever since she was a child. She knew she was talking too much, but she couldn't seem to stem the tide. She was blindingly conscious of the man walking beside her as they climbed stair after stair. He may have been dirty and disheveled, but every inch of his body was perfectly, beautifully proportioned—hard muscles molding a lean and sensuous frame. She was acutely sensitive to the way he moved, to the slight roll of his hips and the pleasantly weary set of his powerful shoulders. His sheer physical presence was unexpectantly riveting. She was astonished by the force of her response to him. She had never been prickly with men; she had always had a light remark on the tip of her tongue and a quick smile ready. But now, suddenly, with this man she felt every inch a woman. A light flirtation had escalated into something very new to her, and she wasn't sure how to deal with it. She felt nervous and strung-up and all-too-conscious of her bedraggled appearance. Tucker would have been appalled. She could almost hear him: "You're not going to impress anyone looking like that, Cookie. Find a pretty dress and I'll take you dancing."

Sam followed her to her door, smiling with enigmatic eyes as Mercy chattered on and on about what a lovely day it had been. She desperately wanted to be alone; she felt like the portrait of Dorian Gray, growing more repulsive looking by the minute.

"Calm down," Sam said kindly, when she finally paused for breath. "You're wasting all kinds of energy that would be better spent on other things."

She flicked a quick, alarmed look at him. "Like what?"

He took the key out of her hand and unlocked the door, ushering her inside. "Like making me a cup of coffee."

"Oh." Mercy felt a stab of something that might have been relief and might have been disappointment. "Of course. Coffee. I'll be right back."

"Mercy?"

She paused on her flight to the kitchen. "What?"

He smiled gently, shrugging his shoulders and pushing his hands into his pockets. "I'm a pretty harmless guy. What you see is what you get."

What she saw was what she got, Mercy thought. Dear heaven, what she saw—his light-filled eyes, so soft and deep and dangerous. The child's sunburn on nose and throat, the colors of sun in his hair . . . and that smile that took her by the heart every time she saw it. No, that didn't reassure her at all.

"Coffee," she muttered, running for the kitchen.

While the coffee maker perked away, she did

what she could to clean up a bit, using the glass oven-front as a mirror. She had no comb for her wind-tangled hair, but did as much as she could with her fingers. At least she could shed her filthy denim jacket and wash her face and hands. She pinched her cheeks for color, then took two cups of coffee into the living room, not daring to risk another glance at herself.

Sam was seated on the sofa, thumbing through a magazine and looking perfectly at home. She gave him his coffee, then sat down gingerly on the opposite end of the sofa like a maiden aunt at a tea party.

"I don't bite," he said, looking at the over-stuffed cushions that separated them.

Mercy was disgusted with the way she was acting, but she couldn't seem to help it. Her entire awareness was focused on him with an almost painful intensity. She absorbed every breath he took, every move he made as though he were nourishment her body had lacked for years and for which it hungered. She hadn't a clue as how to cope with the rush of disturbing sensation. She took a swallow of coffee and burned her tongue. Eyes watering, she put down the cup and grabbed one of the magazines from the coffee table. "I'm not used to having guests here," she said in a husky, breathless voice. "You're my first, as a matter of fact. I've only lived here for a few weeks. I've met a few friends at work, but I haven't had them over because—"

"Why won't you look at me?" Sam interrupted.

"Don't be silly." Her restless, nervous gaze swept over him, then dropped back to the magazine. "I'm looking at you."

"Give me that." He grabbed the magazine out of her hands and tossed it on the floor along with his. Two hours ago he had held her in his arms and all had been right with the world. Now she was all eyes and all nerves, and she couldn't quit fiddling with her hair—smoothing it behind her ears, fluffing up her bangs. "Why can't you relax? What happened between Rock Creek Canyon and here?"

"I'm perfectly relaxed," Mercy replied, giving a little laugh that made her sound like a plugged garbage disposal. "Completely. I'm not . . .

well, I know what I look like. I need to fix my hair, and I could use some lipstick and mascara. I'm not at my best right now, that's all."

Sam shook his head faintly. "What do you mean, you're not at your best? Who told you that you needed lipstick and mascara to be your best?"

She stared at him. "I'm not supposed to say his name."

He drew a long hard breath. "Mercy, you don't need any props or artifice to be at your best. What you *are*—the sweetness, the sensitivity, the spirit—it all comes shining through, regardless of what you look like. The person whose name I cannot say was completely blind, not to mention stupid, if he couldn't see that for himself." He paused, his gaze whimsical yet serious. "You weren't like this with me earlier. Why now? I thought you felt comfortable with me."

"I did," Mercy whispered, nervously twisting a lock of hair around her finger. "But that was before . . ."

He leaned closer, touching her face. "Before what?"

"Before you made me feel things," she said softly, helplessly. She had never felt less capable of expressing herself. "The only person who ever made me feel the way you do was—"

"Shhh." He stopped her with a finger on her lips. Then his hand slipped to the back of her neck and he pulled her forward, inch by inch, until their noses bumped. "We don't say that nasty word, remember? We don't even think about him."

Her expressive mouth quirked at one corner. "Then what do we think about?"

He tipped her nose with a playful kiss. "Oh, we think about pleasant things. Rocky road ice cream. Feather pillows. Starry nights. And, of course, my favorite thing." His next words formed themselves against her softly parted mouth. "Long, slow, deep kisses that last . . . forever . . . and . . . a day."

His lips molded against hers, questing back and forth, altering the kiss in shape and pressure and strength. Like a bee gathering sweet nectar, he suckled and tasted, until they were both trembling. Time slowed, pooling in the shadows of the room, and nothing was heard but the gently arrhythmic sound of their breathing.

His hands began to move, and she was so glad, so *relieved* when he finally lifted and cupped the aching weight of her breasts. She wanted his touch on her, needed the feel of his fingers on her tender flesh. Slowly he pressed her back into the tumbled cushions on the sofa, kisses going on and on like a sweet, sensual feast, his hands shaping her, her hands clinging to his shoulders. Mercy felt with exquisite pleasure the trembling in his body. She wanted to give as much as she received, but she didn't know if it was possible. She'd never known such plenitude, such warmth and communication. Little by little they sank deeper, until Sam's lean body gradually became taut and rigid, and his breath came in hoarse catches in his throat. Finally he pulled back, his skin drenched with heat, his hands balled into tight fists on either side of her head. "That's enough," he said thickly.

Mercy looked at him dazedly, mindless and shivering. Enough? Her body was soft and wet and limp, such a contradiction to the hard, urgent muscles that pressed against her. "It doesn't feel like enough," she whispered through deliciously swollen lips.

He closed his eyes briefly, completing the painful process of bringing himself under control. When he could look at her again, he managed a shaky smile. "If you tried, Mercy

Sullivan, you could drive me out of my mind. You might be able to do it even if you didn't try."

He sat up, watching as she drew herself together. She curled against the end of the sofa, looping her arms around her legs. And all the time she was staring at him, the soft lamplight detailing her face in its innocent hunger.

"Oh, brother," he muttered, looking away from her and taking a steadying breath. His distracted gaze focused on the magazine that had fallen open on the floor. He was looking at the famous Comfort Weave advertisement, a photograph of The Rebel Without a Pause wearing designer briefs and a come-hither smile. The bold headline across the top read, simply, GORGEOUS. "Oh, brother," he said again, in quite a different tone. He snatched up the magazine and closed it, pretending a great interest in the cover. "I haven't read this before," he said. "Do you mind if I take it home with me?"

Her dark eyes opened wide. "You read *Cosmo*?"

"Not all the time," Sam muttered. "But this issue looks kind of interesting. 'Lambada,' 'The Sexy Way To Shape Up' . . . Ten Teeny Bikinis For Not So Teeny Bodies' . . . some good reading material here."

Awkward seconds ticked by as she stared at him. "You're welcome to borrow it," she said finally. "I bought it yesterday and haven't had a chance to look at it yet, but—"

"I'll return it." Sam stood up, moving slowly, running a hand through his tumbled hair. There were so many things he wanted to tell her—he was not a crazy person who dressed like a cowboy and read *Cosmo*. He simply wanted to buy a little more time with her, that was all. He wanted to be Just Sam as long as he could because when all was said and done, that's all he had to offer. And he wished to heaven he could stay with her, but he couldn't. It wouldn't have been fair to her. She was caught between what was and what could be.

But words were never easy when two people were cautiously finding their way with each other. It was easier to say too little than too much. He was frightened of hurting her, he was frightened of being hurt himself. He stared at her gravely, then leaned over and kissed the top of her head, his palm shaping the curve of her cheek.

"Thank you for my day," he said softly. His eyes said so much more to her, but her head was bent, and she was staring at her hands clasped in her lap. "Good night, Mercy."

She looked up as soon as he turned away from her, her gaze following him to the door. "Sam?"

He looked over his shoulder, his hand on the doorknob. "Yes?"

She cuddled into the cushions, her knees up and close to her body. "I don't know your last name. You never told me."

There was a long pause. His smile was slow in coming. "I must have overlooked it," he said. Then he winked at her and closed the door behind him.

In the bright, white light of Monday morning, Mercy's mind was working somewhat more effectively than it had the previous night. She understood or thought she did, Sam's reasons for leaving so abruptly. He was a caring and honest man who refused to take advantage of her emotional turmoil. Whatever happened between them while she was struggling to resolve her emotional ties to Tucker Healy would have no validity. Still, she was a little piqued that Sam had been able to bring the situation under control so easily. He might have slipped a little, exhibited a fraction of the frustration that she had felt. Even now, after twelve hours and a cool shower, her skin prickled with a heated awareness.

She dressed for work in white knit leggings, comfortable ballet shoes, and an oversize silky sweatshirt that reached to her knees. After nearly three weeks of working as a personal assistant to one of Denver's foremost commercial photographers, Mercy had learned that how she looked was secondary to how well she could move in whatever she wore. Could she climb to the top of a ladder without splitting a seam or exposing her unmentionables? Could she reach and stretch and duck with her arms full of lights and cords and camera equipment? Most important, could she stay on her feet for eight to ten hours at a stretch, running this way and that way while Tommy Evans barked orders and made up new four-letter words to match his mood? This was Mercy's first experience dealing with the "artistic temperament," and she'd certainly had her eyes opened. In New York, she had worked for a photography studio that specialized in taking school pictures of elementary-age students. It was a job that required more patience than ingenuity, more endurance than talent. Working for Tommy Evans was something else altogether. He was a man of strong opinions, sharp edges, and fiery mood swings. Mercy had been told he was also a genius, but she was withholding judgment on that. She really wasn't familiar with the tricks and triumphs of commercial photography. Her job in New York had been small potatoes; she was small potatoes in Denver, but she was working for a man with an international reputation. She was nothing more than a glorified gofer, but the pay wasn't bad and every once in a while Evans twisted his lips into what might have been a smile and told her she was "coming right along." Although Mercy wasn't interested in a career in product advertising, she knew she could learn a great deal from the man. Hopefully one day she would have the qualifications and experience to branch out on her own as a fashion photographer.

This particular morning, Tommy's studio was in more of an uproar than usual. Mercy cornered Judith Passco, Tommy's set designer, in the conference room and asked her jokingly if Mel Gibson was scheduled for a shoot.

"Someone as good," Judith said, pressing her hand over her heart and fluttering her false eyelashes. "The Rebel Without a Pause is baring his manly chest for us today. We're shooting a Second Skin jeans ad. I've been palpitating all morning, anticipating all that lovely muscle and sinew. You know how luscious those Second Skin ads can be—very hot stuff."

"The rebel without a what?"

"Darling, you need to get out more. The only people you recognize are involved in baseball"— she sniffed disdainfully—"and that's because of that mucho macho ex-fiancé of yours. It's a pity, it truly is. You've never heard of The Rebel Without a Pause?"

Mercy shrugged. "I've heard the phrase. Isn't he some race car driver or something?"

"You're hopeless," Judith wailed. "That baseball player absolutely ruined you. Go upstairs and feast your eyes on the most gorgeous man in the world, dear heart. You have a lot of deprivation to make up for."

"He's here now?" Mercy was interested but hardly ecstatic. She was preoccupied with an empty, tugging sensation deep inside that told her she was missing Sam. Wondering where he was, what he was doing, if he was thinking about her. She was hesitant to concentrate on the feeling—the old "knock on wood" syndrome. She had become sexually aware of him overnight, and the feeling might pass as quickly as it had come.

But somehow she didn't think so.

At Judith's urging, she went upstairs to Makeup, where the most gorgeous man in the world was being primped and polished. She opened the door and peeped in, intending to slip right out again as soon as she "feasted her eyes." Mr. Gorgeous was up to his neck in pink plastic, sitting in a beautician's chair with his back to Mercy. The hair stylist was fussing over him with a comb in one hand and a can of hairspray in the other, the makeup artist was dabbing at his cheeks with a huge brush and chattering on in a breathy voice about ageless bone structure. In the corner of the room, Tommy, his assistant cameraman, and his art director were huddled together in a ferocious planning session, all three talking at once. Soothing classical music was being piped through the intercom system, for all the good it did.

Tommy spotted Mercy out of the corner of his eye. "You there! I need you. We're almost ready here. Go downstairs to the studio and check the lights. Have you seen Judith around?"

"She's in the conference room," Mercy replied, stepping partially out from behind the door. "At least she was five minutes ago."

"Tell her I need to see her, stat."

Tommy waved her away and went back to his conversation. As she turned to leave, Mercy slanted a quick look at the reflection in the mirror on the opposite wall. She saw professionally windswept hair, every blond strand coaxed into place. A very pretty helmet, she thought, hiding a smile. Her eyes flicked over the rest of his face, noting those ageless cheekbones, Newman-blue eyes, and a square jaw that would photograph just as well as Mel Gibson's. She met his light-filled eyes in the mirror and smiled rather vaguely, then closed the door.

And then opened it again, with enough force to bury the doorknob in the wall.

"*Sam?*" Her voice was pitched somewhere between a gasp and a shriek, but it was loud enough to draw all eyes.

Sam didn't move, he didn't even blink. He hadn't twitched a muscle since Mercy had walked into the room the first time, and he had realized what a nasty joke fate had played on him. He wanted to toss his pink plastic bib-thing over his head and hide.

"Yes, Mercy, that's Sam Christie," Tommy drawled sarcastically. "Isn't it amazing, considering the fact we're photographing him today? Get a grip, lady. We're professionals here, remember? This is no time for heart palpitations."

Mercy barely heard him. She walked slowly across the room, whipping the beautician's chair in a half circle with both hands. A myriad of impressions scurried through her mind—he was wearing more makeup than she was, his hair had been trimmed, his expression was frozen as if he'd been struck by lightning.

"You could use a little more blush," Mercy said in a shaky, brittle voice. "And maybe a touch of lip gloss. You want to look your best, don't you?"

"I can explain," Sam said.

"The makeup base is good, though. I like that touch of apricot—very natural on you. And that hair . . . goodness, that style should last you until Halloween."

Sam tried to fight his way out of the plastic drape. "If you'd just listen to me—"

"I have work to do," Mercy said. "It was a thrill meeting you, Mr. Christie." She turned on her heel and walked out the door without a backward glance. She could hear Sam shouting at Tommy and Tommy shouting at someone else, but she didn't really care. Sam Christie. She had seen him in television commercials, she had read about him in gossip magazines, she had even watched him win two gold medals in the Winter Olympics seven years earlier. But somehow she had never connected Sam Christie's face with the sticky invalid who had passed out on the floor of the elevator in her apartment building. A person didn't expect to meet celebrities that way.

She met Judith on the stairs and told her that Tommy wanted to see her. Then she kept right on walking, out the front door and down the sidewalk. She had no idea where she was going, but she had to keep moving. She put one foot in front of the other, her mind whirling. She tried desperately to search her character for some flaw, some error in judgment that had led to her becoming involved with the notorious Rebel Without a Pause. How ironic . . . she was such a simple soul. She had never wanted anything more than peace and security. A painful feeling ripped through her, and she sat down abruptly on the bench at the corner bus stop.

She couldn't believe this had happened to her . . . again. For so many years there had been only one man in her life—Tucker, the prince turned to a toad. He thrived on being in the limelight, the irrepressible all-American boy who broke hearts almost accidentally with dazzling guileless charm. She had catered to his whims, his smiles, his excuses, until she had nothing left to give. Leaving him had been the hardest thing she had ever done, and she still wasn't sure where she had found the courage. She only knew that she never wanted to love like that again, chasing rainbows, waiting for a happy-every-after that never came.

But then came Sam.

Good neighbor Sam, who extolled the virtues of being yourself. He reminded her there were tender moments to be found. He made her laugh. He gave her thrills and chills. He dove headfirst into swamp water. He inspired hungers and cravings she hadn't known she was capable of. In three short days, he had convinced her that princes did exist, damn him, damn him, damn him. Unfortunately, he wasn't a prince. He wasn't even a toad. Sam Christie's reputation was that of a man who sought pleasure wherever he could find it. He only *impersonated* a normal, humble, caring human being. He probably did it for kicks. *Hi there, I'm just a sweet country boy who grew up on a potato farm . . .*

"Hi, there," Sam said quietly.

He was standing directly in front of her. Mercy kept her eyes firmly at belt-buckle height. "Go away, Sam. I don't like you anymore."

He sat down beside her, head bent, elbows resting on his knees. "Yes, you do."

She scowled at him. "No, I don't. I don't even know you."

"Look, give me a chance to explain. I wanted to tell you, but—"

"Then why didn't you? How hard is it to say, 'By the way, I'm famous. I won two gold medals in the Olympics and I pose in my underwear and I make American Express commercials and I have affairs with starlets and centerfold models—'"

"The hell I do!"

She subsided into silence. She rather thought that last bit might have been an exaggeration on the part of the tabloids. They sat, stiff and tense, the wooden bench a painful oasis of silence amidst the noises of the city: horns honking, cars zipping by, the wail of a police siren.

"I never lied to you," Sam said suddenly.

She didn't look at him.

"It's true," he insisted quietly. "You met the real Sam Christie. Everything we shared was real. That guy back in the photography studio . . . he's not my soul mate, Mercy. He's an image the public has of me. I have to live with him, I figure I can dispose of him any way I choose."

"You better get out of the sun," Mercy said stubbornly, tears pooling in her eyes. "Your mascara will run."

"I'm not wearing bloody mascara, and you know it!" Sam took her by the shoulders with both hands, forcing her to look at him. "Once upon a time, I skied down a mountain faster than anyone else and I won medals for it. After that, some jackass journalists dubbed me The Rebel Without a Pause, and fool that I was, I wasted a few years of my life trying to live up to that reputation. Eventually reality set in. My knees went bad, I had to retire from racing, and I finally realized that we all have to grow up sooner or later. I'm not ashamed of what I do now. The people I care about know the difference between the image and the man."

Words, words, words, Mercy thought. Tucker had been very good with words too. She turned her head away from him, though his fingers dug into her shoulders. "Let me go. People are staring."

"People always stare at a familiar face. I've learned to live with it."

"I'm so happy for you."

"Dammit, Mercy, will you listen to me?" His

voice was soft, but he spoke each word with individual intensity. "I'm the same man who laughed with you yesterday, I'm the same man who held you in his arms last night. Nothing has changed, nothing at all."

"You're wrong," she said. "Everything has changed."

"Only if you let it."

Mercy sniffed furiously. "You said you grew up on a potato farm. I can't believe I fell for that!"

"I did grow up on a potato farm, dammit!"

"You said you were a salesman."

"I am. I'm a spokesman for a sporting goods company. I endorse different products, I make commercials. I sell the image people have of Sam Christie."

Then, in a dull voice she said, "You said you were harmless."

He brought her face to his once again. "I am," he said quietly, the faintest hint of bitterness in his tone. "That's the hell of all this. I've never met your illustrious fiancé, but somehow I get the feeling I'm being held accountable for the pain he caused you. I don't deserve that, Mercy. He had his chance and he blew it."

"Excuse me . . . aren't you Sam Christie? Would you mind giving me your autograph, please?"

A stunning blond woman was standing in front of them, holding out a pen and paper. Her cropped hair was artfully arranged in somewhat the same windswept style as Sam's, and her zebra-stripe pantsuit might have been painted on her voluptuous figure. Mercy closed her eyes briefly, remembering all the times she had acted out this particular scene with Tucker. It had always been the same, Mercy fading into the background while Tucker turned on the charm and obliged the pretty lady. And Mercy had been *such* a good sport, telling herself Tucker had no choice but to cater to the fans, telling herself she was imagining the subtle, sexual messages coming and going between Tucker and the female population at large.

Well, she didn't feel like being a good sport now. She sat in brittle silence while Sam, scribbled something on the paper and handed it back to the zebra woman. She thanked him profusely, thanked him again, then looked at Mercy for the very first time.

"Oh," she said, pencil-thin brows drawing together. "Hello, there. Are you . . . someone?"

Mercy stood up, tangled emotions forming a steaming haze inside her mind. "Absolutely not," she said. "Just another hopelessly devoted fan. Take my seat, won't you? The two of you can have a nice chat. Good-bye, Mr. Christie. I wish you all the best."

She stalked down the sidewalk, head held high, heart lodged like a stone in the pit of her stomach. She looked back on the events of the past few days with an almost detached curiosity, wondering what she had done to deserve this ironic twist of fate. She wanted mediocrity, that's what she wanted. She wanted an uncomplicated life, a quiet life. When and if she ever fell in love again, she had visualized it would be with an honest, hard-working bank teller, or perhaps a soft-spoken piano tuner . . . someone sweet and kind and completely anonymous, someone who would look at Mercy Rose Sullivan and see the moon and the stars shining in her eyes. Turning from Tucker Healy to a man like Sam Christie was like jumping from a frying pan into a boiling volcano.

She was such a simple soul. Was it too much to ask to want to meet someone who had never been on the cover of a national magazine? Someone who had a receding hair-line or a pot belly? *Where were all the damn piano tuners, for Pete's sake?*

She had no idea she'd said the words out loud until she heard Sam's irritated voice behind her.

"What do you mean, where are all the piano turners? You are the strangest girl. Will you please slow down?"

She glanced over her shoulder, at the same time increasing her pace. "Stop following me. Go away. Shoo."

"*Shoo?*"

She didn't miss the amusement in his voice, and it made her even angrier. "I don't have time for this. I have to get back to work."

He jogged a few steps, catching up to her.

"So do I, remember? I have a job, the same as you do. I have to pay bills and taxes and keep my employers happy, the same as you do."

"I see. You're an ordinary guy who wants to do his job. Fine."

Sam tried to take her hand, and she whipped it away. He sighed, looking at the uncompromising set of her shoulders. "You're not going to make this easy, are you?"

"Of course I'm going to make it easy. It's my job to make sure every shoot goes smoothly, and I'm very good at it."

"I wasn't talking about the shoot, and you know it." He followed her up the steps to the studio, lightly slapping her hand away from the door when she tried to open it. "I'm also a gentleman," he said, opening the door for her and standing back. "Just an old-fashioned kind of guy."

Mercy stopped dead at the threshold, staring at the little crowd gathered in the reception room. Tommy, Judith, everyone from the makeup room, even the building's custodian; all wearing identical expressions of bemused curiosity.

"Mr. Christie needed a little fresh air," she muttered. "We're back now."

"I see," Tommy said in a tone that indicated he didn't see at all. "Well, then . . . good. Time is money, so let's get down to it, shall we? Sam?"

"Of course, as soon as I have a minute alone with Mercy." Sam smiled at one and all over

Mercy's shoulder as he caught hold of the back of her sweatshirt. "We haven't quite finished our conversation. I hope you don't mind?"

Everyone looked at Tommy. After a moment's hesitation, Tommy summoned an understanding smile. "Of course we don't mind. We'll be waiting for you in the studio."

Sam kept a firm hold on Mercy's sweatshirt as the room emptied. The moment they were alone, she twisted out of his grip, turning on him with blazing eyes. "You're going to get me fired! Is that what you want?"

"Of course not. That would be cruel."

"Then leave me alone."

He smiled. "No. I don't want to leave you alone. I want to take you to dinner tonight."

"Absolutely not."

"I'll pick you up at seven. Literally, figuratively . . . it's up to you."

She lifted her chin another inch, and her lips pursed ominously. "You can try."

It was too much to resist. He planted a hard, smacking kiss on her lips. "I love a challenge. Let's get back to work, pumpkin. You know what Tommy said—time is money. We can talk later."

"You're not a well person," she said, the words passing haltingly through kiss-numbed lips.

"I know." He gave her his pirate's grin. "Damn, but you're cute."

Mercy watched him in a bewildered way as he turned and walked away from her. She

continued to stare idiotically at the door leading to the studio long after Sam had disap-
peared through it. She felt a nagging ache in
the back of her head.

It was going to be a long day.

Five

"Oh, my goodness . . . have you ever . . . look at his . . . well, I never . . . but I wish I had . . ."

Judith was having some sort of an attack. Mercy patted her on the back automatically, never taking her eyes from the riveting scene in the studio. A bedroom set had been constructed, a moody room done in black and white, deliberately cluttered to give it that "helpless bachelor" look. Sam was stretched out on the bed, wearing his Second Skin jeans and a haunting smile. His legs were crossed at the ankles, his feet were bare, and both his hands idly gripped the headboard above his head. A single candle burned on the bedside table, smoothing golden light over his skin like oil.

"Brood," Tommy instructed him, clicking

YOU GET SIX
ROMANCES RISK FREE...
Plus AN EXCLUSIVE TITLE FREE!

Loveswept Romances

AFFIX
RISK FREE
BOOKS
STAMP
HERE.

Kay Hooper's
**Larger
Than
Life**

This FREE gift
is yours to keep.

MY "NO RISK" GUARANTEE

There's no obligation to buy and the free gift is mine to keep. I may preview each
subsequent shipment for 15 days. If I don't want it, I simply return the books
within 15 days and owe nothing. If I keep them, I will pay just $2.25 per book. I
save $3.00 off the retail price for the 6 books (plus postage and handling, and
sales tax in NY).

YES! Please send my six Loveswept novels
RISK FREE along with my FREE GIFT
described inside the heart!   **RA123**   41228

NAME_____

ADDRESS_____APT_____

CITY_____

STATE_____ZIP_____

away with his Nikon. "Brood like hell. That's it . . . good. Good."

"He's *brooding*," Judith whispered hoarsely, clutching Mercy's arm. "I have never, ever seen anyone with such charisma. How will I ever be able to face poor Ralph tonight after lusting after another man this way? I'm so ashamed of myself."

Mercy fought down an impulse to slap her hand over Judith's eyes. Every muscle in her body was taut. She was utterly miserable with a mind-boggling combination of jealousy, antagonism, and helplessness. Judith's hot and bothered commentary wasn't helping the situation. "Maybe you should go downstairs," she said, managing a tight little smile.

"No. I'm not *that* ashamed." Judith pursed her lips, whistling soundlessly. "What a gorgeous man. Ralph used to have a tummy like that, back in eighty-six, I think. Ah, well. It doesn't matter where you get your appetite, as long as you eat at home. Mercy dear, when are you going to tell me what's going on between you and the sexiest man on earth? It's not nice to leave me guessing, it's really not."

"I already explained." Mercy plucked at her sweatshirt, feeling uncomfortably warm. "We live in the same apartment building. We met in the elevator a couple of days ago. I hardly know him, Judith." There was a short pause before she said abruptly, "I think Tommy's making these pictures a little suggestive, don't you? We're not after blatant sexuality here."

"Sourpuss," Judith chided. "Why shouldn't women be able to enjoy a little harmless fantasizing? We're not all as fortunate as you are, honeychild. You have the real thing."

"I told you, Sam and I are just—"

"Friends. I know. Look there, he's stretching out on his side. Oh, isn't that cute, the way he cuddles that pillow?" Judith sighed, tipping her head sideways to better appreciate the view. "All right, Mercy. Keep your secrets. I suppose if I were in your shoes, I'd keep a low profile too. Being involved with a man like Sam Christie couldn't be easy, not with every red-blooded woman in America dying to take your place."

"Mercy, get some mood music going here," Tommy called. Then, belatedly he added, "If you would, please."

Tommy hadn't quite figured out how his lowly assistant and Sam Christie knew each other, but he wasn't taking any chances. He had used the magic word more than once when giving Mercy instructions, each time glancing over at Sam to gauge his reaction. But Sam was a pro at giving nothing away, and Mercy was still in a state of shock and confusion. Those who had witnessed the little scene in the makeup room were professional enough to keep their opinions to themselves, although they did have a speculative gleam in their eyes whenever they looked in Mercy's direction.

Mercy walked over to the stereo system and pushed in a tape with shaking fingers. A few seconds later, the sounds of mellow jazz filtered through the studio. Music fit for brooding, she thought, though she wasn't sure how much more brooding she could take before she went into cardiac arrest. Her breathing was erratic, her skin flushed. She felt as if she were coming down with something. Her mouth was dry, her stomach wrenched.

She looked at Sam and found his gaze focused on her, his pale blond hair drifting around his head like a halo in the soft lights. His smile was faint, and only for her. There was something mesmerizing about his features, but when she tried to put her finger on what it was, definition was elusive. It wasn't a handsome face, yet the refined tenderness he radiated was captivating. She could understand why female hearts beat faster when women tried to imagine what thoughts went on behind his sweet, boyish grin and hot silver-blue eyes. His was a face built for sweetness; combined with an athletic body that was superbly endowed, long-limbed, graceful. The total effect carried the power of chain lightning.

Mercy tore her gaze away from him and walked slowly back to Judith, planting herself like a burr against the white stucco wall. Yearnings and fears were swelling in her, bursting, flowing downward through stinging paths. She wondered with a strange detachment if it showed on her face, this painful sensual awareness. Judith was chattering on about heart palpitations, but her tone was light and teasing. No matter how Mercy tried, she couldn't stop the pain in her muscles of wanting him. The feelings were too powerful, like a drug spreading a fiery magic through her system. Judith's enthusiastic appreciation of the man in the Second Skin jeans was becoming unbearable. Mercy wished she could fold up inside herself and disappear. She was amazed how close she was to tears.

"How long do you think this will take?" she asked Judith suddenly, her voice very low.

Judith sighed and grinned and shook her head. "I really don't know. All day, I hope. All night. All day tomorrow . . ."

Mercy closed her eyes briefly, and the sound that caught in her throat resembled a whimper. She couldn't stand it anymore. She felt radioactive. She chanced another look at Sam, and found her eyes helplessly tangled up with his once again. His look was as serious as she had ever seen it. The message he sent her was clear. He knew. Everything she thought, everything she felt.

Tommy asked Sam to turn sideways, and their silent communication was cut off. Mercy inhaled deeply, for the first time in hours. At least it felt like hours.

She turned to Judith in a sudden, almost startled movement. "Judith . . . I think I need to go home early today. I don't feel well."

Immediately Judith's dreamy expression changed to one of genuine concern. "Are you all right? Would you like a ride home?"

"I'll get a cab, thanks. Tell Tommy for me when he's finished the shoot, will you?"

Judith nodded, looking sorrowful. "Of course I will. You must be feeling absolutely terrible to be willing to walk out on scenery like this. Are you sure there's nothing I can do for you?"

"Not a thing, really. I'll see you tomorrow." Mercy began to move unobtrusively toward the door. Immediately Sam looked up. It was as if some part of him had been focused on her the entire time, so that he knew every move she made the moment she made it.

"Mercy?" he said.

All heads turned in her direction. Mercy swallowed hard, feeling another hiccup attack coming on. "Yes, Mr. Christie?"

"You're looking a little pale, *Ms.* Sullivan. Are you all right?"

Mercy addressed her reply to Tommy. "Actually, I'm not feeling well. Do you mind if I go home early?"

Tommy looked almost relieved. "Not at all. Take the rest of the day off, please. I'm sure we can manage without you for a few hours."

"I hope you'll be feeling better by tonight," Sam put in innocently.

Mercy held his gaze. "I won't be."

He smiled. "Think positively. Maybe by . . . seven o'clock? I think you'll be better by then, don't you?"

"No," Mercy snapped. "I will still be sick at seven o'clock. You can count on it."

Softly Sam said, "Then I'll have to make you feel better, won't I?"

Judith suddenly had a choking fit. Mercy slapped her none too gently on the back until she seemed to be breathing normally again. Then she shrugged to the room at large and fled.

She didn't start to hiccup until she was in a cab on the way home.

At six-thirty, Mercy took a long, hot shower, dressed in a completely shapeless quilted robe and wrapped a terrycloth turban around her wet hair. She wore not a speck of makeup, and smelled of nothing more alluring than soap. Even the most optimistic man would recognize a woman who had no intention of going out for the evening.

She paced the living room and watched the clock above the mantel. She was too nervous to sit still. Amidst the confusion that jangled within her, she wondered sadly why something that had felt so good could have turned out to be so very wrong for her.

Sam knocked softly on the door at ten minutes to seven.

Had she lived on the first floor instead of the fourth, Mercy might have succumbed to the impulse to jump out the bedroom window and run for her life. As it was, she could only tighten the belt on her ugly robe and open the door.

If he was surprised at her appearance, Sam

gave no sign of it. He smiled sweetly and handed her a huge, heart-shape box of chocolates. "I must be a little early," he said, giving her a quick kiss on the cheek.

Before she could protest, he was inside the apartment, shrugging out of his leather bomber jacket and tossing it over the back of a chair. He wore a cream-color sweater and brown pleated slacks that looked as though he might have ironed them himself. His hair was nicely disheveled, there was a razor nick on his chin, and he smelled of Old Spice. There wasn't a hint of the infamous Rebel Without a Pause.

A good disguise, Mercy thought, pushing the drooping turban out of her eyes. Ordinary, comfortable, harmless . . . but she knew better.

"Won't you come in?" she said sarcastically as he made himself at home on the sofa.

"Thank you." Something that might have been amusement flickered in his eyes. "I apologize for being early, but I got tired of standing out in the hall."

Mercy stared at him. "What do you mean, you got tired of standing in the hall?"

"I thought you might run away again. You do have that tendency, you know. I've been hanging around outside your door since six o'clock." He folded his hands in his lap and assumed a repentant expression. "I didn't trust you. I'm ashamed of myself, and terribly sorry."

Mercy took a deep breath, clutching the

chocolates to her chest. "I had no intention of avoiding you tonight."

His beautiful smile broke through. "That's nice."

"I have no intention of going with you, either."

His face fell. "For a minute there, I thought this was going to be simple. Come and sit by me, Mercy. Let's explore your inconsistencies."

Self-preservation reared its startled head. "Absolutely not. My mind is made up, Sam, no matter what the other parts of me might . . ." Mistake, she thought. "My mind is made up," she finished lamely.

"I see." He studied her with bright blue eyes. "Mercy Sullivan, you're a chicken."

"I'm not scared," Mercy shot back, her turban tumbling to the floor as she tossed her head. "I'm realistic. I'm smart. I know me, and I know people like you."

"People like me," Sam murmured, staring at her as he scratched his chin thoughtfully. "I wonder what that means? I wasn't aware there *were* any other people like me. I know I've never met anyone else like you before. I always figured we were all individuals and should be judged accordingly."

Mercy's wet hair dangled over her eyes. She shook it back, wishing he would take his intense light-filled gaze and put it somewhere else. "I always figured we should learn by our mistakes and try not to repeat them."

Sam made a face. "I'm getting those nasty

Tucker vibrations again." He stood up and glanced around the room in a restless fashion, then slowly walked to the window. His broad shoulders were dramatic outlined against the fiery Colorado sunset. After what seemed an endless silence, he turned, met her gaze, and said softly, "I want to be with you, Mercy. Do you want to be with me?"

Don't do this, she wanted to beg him. *Don't be sweet and disarming and sexy and make me forget all the good reasons I have for sending you away.* "I'm sorry," she whispered. "It would be too complicated."

He tilted his head curiously. "Why? I mean, is this based on something concrete and logical, or are we back to the 'I can't possibly have a relationship with you because you pose in your underwear' doctrine?"

His tone was light and teasing, yet she heard a subtle undercurrent of anxiety. She realized with a little shock that she was actually capable of hurting this beautiful, sexy, self-assured man who had the world at his feet. The fact that he was vulnerable to Mercy Rose Sullivan amazed and touched her.

She didn't want to hurt him. On the other hand, she didn't want to be hurt, either. Confused and torn as she was, she could only stand there and stare at him, helplessly caught in the dancing light she saw in his eyes.

"I'm harmless," he said cajolingly. "A sweet country boy with nothing more serious on his mind than sharing a good meal with a pretty lady."

That almost made her smile. "Sam Christie, a sweet country boy?"

"That's right. Just your ordinary potato farmer. I'd love to show you some old-fashioned Western hospitality, ma'am. Could I please take you out for supper?"

Mercy felt the last of her determination slip away like sand in an hourglass. "You're not going to give up, are you?" she said somewhat irritably, though all the while a strange spirit within her was jumping and shouting for joy.

"I doubt it," Sam said. "At least not in this lifetime."

He took a step toward her. Instinctively Mercy stepped back, because everything was moving too quickly for her. In her heart she knew she was going to follow a course that she could very well regret. She also knew she didn't have the strength to resist.

"It might be chemistry," she said defensively. "This thing with us. A chemical reaction."

Sam nodded, blue eyes twinkling. "And we might be kidnapped by one-eyed, one-eared, giant purple people-eaters on our way to dinner. Hurry and get dressed, Mercy-mine. I'm hungry."

He endowed the last word with a husky emphasis that Mercy chose to ignore. She gave him one last confused scowl and left the room.

While she was drying her hair, she pondered on the proper attire for a date with the sexiest potato farmer in the world. She scoured her closet, pulling forth a drop-dead little black dress that revealed everything but her birthmark. Then, with a sudden spirit of mischief, she decided the "drop-dead" look was all wrong for an evening of old-fashioned Western hospitality. She dug out her oldest jeans and a fitted Western-style shirt with a lace-trimmed yoke she had worn in a high-school production of *Oklahoma*. As a finishing touch, she tugged on a pair of bright red boots with sassy little tassels on the heels. Now she was a suitable companion for a sweet country boy.

When she walked back into the living room, Sam was once again standing at the window. She made a soft "ahem," rocking up and down on the heels of her boots as he turned to gaze at her. "Howdy. Ready to go?"

He hesitated, obviously taken aback. "You look like Annie Oakley," he said huskily, his gaze following the sweet curve of her hips.

Mercy shot him a saucy smile, tossing back her dark hair. "I figured you'd like this outfit, since you're such a down-home type yourself."

Sam grinned, looking at his Gucci loafers. "Oh . . . yeah. Well, tonight I thought I'd try a new look. Still, you've inspired me. Now I know exactly where to take you for dinner."

She frowned suspiciously, visions of truck stops dancing through her head. "Really? Where?"

"That's for me to know and you to adjust to. Come along, Annie. Time's a-wasting."

He didn't touch her until they were safely in the Jeep. He didn't dare to, not with all his senses clamoring and the perspiration breaking out on his brow. Longing repeatedly shuddered through him like the backlash of a powerful wave. At the same time, an odd, feathery peace settled deep within him, strangely compatible with the restless stirrings of his body. It was the most complete feeling he had ever known.

But once their seat belts were buckled and they were zipping along the freeway at seventy miles an hour, he permitted himself to take her hand.

Holding hands. He'd never considered it a sexual act. But with her dark-lashed eyes shining like stars and her sweet, husky voice surrounding him like an erotic lullaby, holding hands become something quite extraordinary. His fingers laced through hers, his thumb lightly stroking the side of her hand. Worshiping. Hypnotizing. Her fingers began to tremble and to curl against his palm. His grip tightened instinctively, feeling the warmth of her hand spread up his arm, melting the tenseness of his shoulder muscles. If she could do this to him with the touch of her small hand, what would it be like if they . . . when they . . .

Oh, Mercy.

Holding hands, Mercy thought. It had been so long since a man had taken her hand. She had been guided with a hand on her back, led with a hand on her elbow, pulled along with a hand over her wrist. This was so different. This sweet, simple gesture was a meeting, not a domination, a shared pleasure, a tantalizing hint of the power of his touch. Her hand seemed to be developing a highly charged life of its own, tingling, warming, pulsing with sensitivity. She closed her eyes, concentrating on the feeling. She would be content if they drove forever, just holding hands.

Liar, an inner voice teased. You want more. So much more . . .

He took her to The Sundowner, a Western-style honky-tonk in the heart of the city, complete with a live band and an old-fashioned hardwood dance floor. It seemed that every man in the place—with the exception of Sam—was wearing cowboy boots and silver belt-buckles the size of turkey platters. The women were dressed the same way as Mercy was, and she felt right at home—until she read the menu.

"I don't recognize most of these entrees," she said finally. "Prairie Oysters. I've never heard of prairie oysters. What are they?"

Sam grinned with bright-eyed innocence. "Order them and find out. Live dangerously."

"I'm perfectly willing to live dangerously," she said, batting her eyelashes at Sam over the top of the menu. "But I refuse to eat dangerously. What are they?"

He consulted his menu. "It says here, if you have to ask, then don't order them."

"Sam—"

"All right, you asked for it." He set his menu on the table and regarded her gravely. "There is no delicate way to put this, Annie. Prairie oysters are . . . the best of the bull."

It took her a moment to absorb this. "You've got to be kidding. Well, that's disgusting. I'll have beans and weenies. At least I know what they are."

Sam lifted one skeptical brow. "Are you sure? They can be kind of tricky here, sweetheart."

Mercy ordered chili-spiced chicken strips and cheese spuds. Sam had rib-eye steak and barbecued beans. Conversation grew sparse as the meal progressed, the looks between them more lingering. Mercy felt as if her senses were on overload. Goosebumps pebbled her arms, and her breath was catching high in her chest. By the time dessert arrived, they couldn't tear their eyes off each other.

It was Sam who pushed his plate away and stood up, offering Mercy his hand. "Dance with me," he said hoarsely. He needed to have her near to him—*now*. Other than ducking outside and making out in the Jeep like oversexed teenagers, dancing seemed to be his only immediate option.

Mercy followed Sam to the crowded dance floor and went into his arms. He pulled her close, his chin brushing the top of her head. The music had slowed to a country ballad, which was fortunate since Mercy was too unsettled to concentrate much on fancy footwork. There were too many other parts of her body buzzing for attention. As they swayed almost imperceptibly against each other, she had the sensation that the voices around them were fading, the music, the people drifting away. They were alone. Mercy's eyes slowly closed, a shiver running through her as he touched his lips to her neck. She couldn't hear the music. Her feet slowed with his, until they were sharing more of an embrace than a dance. She turned her head and rubbed her lips over the pulse at the base of his throat. He groaned deep in his chest, his hands slipping downward to cup her buttocks. Mercy cuddled herself against him like a drowsy kitten, seeking his warmth, curving herself into his thighs. It felt so good to be next to him. What would it feel like to be part of him?

Neither of them heard the music stop. They held each other until a hand tapped Sam insistently on his shoulder. A giggling woman with a shock of freshly permed yellow hair asked him for his autograph.

Sam's teeth were clenched together so hard, he thought he might crack a filling, but he managed to smile as he signed the napkin she gave him. Someone else approached him, and before long, he was surrounded by fans. He chatted away and smiled and signed autographs, and when the music started up again, he found himself swept up in a dance with a middle-aged woman wearing a Stetson and a huge turquoise Indian necklace over her plaid shirt. He took two turns around the floor with her, then, when he was about to excuse himself and return to Mercy at their table, another woman cut in. She was quite a bit younger than his first partner, sporting Cleopatra eye makeup and a low-cut peasant blouse that barely contained her ample proportions. As a matter of fact, she was spilling out everywhere, and for the life of him, Sam couldn't see a safe way to hold her.

He decided not to try. "I'm sorry," he said. "I'd love to dance, but I'm neglecting my date. Another time."

"I'm free later tonight," Cleopatra offered in a throaty voice. "All . . . night . . . long. I'd love to see if you really live up to your reputation, Sam Christie."

Normally Sam handled these situations with the ease born of experience, knowing when to charm his way out of a scene, knowing when to keep his distance. This night, however, he was distracted by the dark-eyed brunette shooting daggers at him from a table fifteen feet away. He watched with a sinking heart as Mercy stood up and began walking toward them. "This isn't good," he muttered to himself, shaking Cleo's hand off his arm.

But the persistent woman rose up on tiptoes and whispered into his ear. "My name is Barbara. Let me give you my phone number. You can call anytime, night or day. I promise you won't be sorry, Sam Christie."

"But you'll be sorry," Mercy said from behind them. "If you don't back off, you're going to be *so* sorry . . ."

Sam looked from Mercy's diminutive figure to Barbara's Amazonian proportions, then rolled his eyes toward heaven. "Mercy, I was just coming to get you. This is Barbara, Barbara, this is Mercy. Well, it's getting late. We should be on our way, Mercy."

Barbara snorted, her expression hostile. "Yegads. I'll never understand what men see in these little Milquetoast types."

"It's obvious what men see in you," Mercy replied with baby-doll innocence, looking pointedly at the other woman's chest.

"Time to go," Sam said quickly, taking Mercy's arm. "Not a minute to lose."

Mercy shook him off, holding her ground. She didn't like this woman who had felt so free to proposition her man. Yes, *her man*. If there had been any doubt about it before, there wasn't any longer. She felt an almost primitive urge to protect her territory. It was something quite new to her, and altogether uncharacteristic for mild-mannered Mercy Rose. She had no doubt that Sam was capable of taking care of himself, but that wasn't the issue. This was between two women. "Take a hint," she said. "The man isn't interested, *Babs*."

Barbara gave a short, strident laugh. "Boy, do you have a lot to learn. Men are always interested, honey."

A small crowd had quickly grown to a large crowd. A flashbulb went off in Sam's face, and he swore softly, blinking away the sunspots exploding behind his eyes. "Mercy, I think we've overstayed our welcome here."

"Not as far as I'm concerned," Barbara said throatily, tickling Sam beneath his chin and watching Mercy through the corner of her eye. "Stick around, Sam Christie. I'll show you what a warm welcome really can be. I'll bet little Miss Mercy gives you frostbite when you cuddle up."

Mercy couldn't stop herself. For the first time in her life, she was provoked to physical violence. She whipped back her hand to slap the woman across the face, only to have Sam grab her wrist in midswing.

"No, you don't," he said. "You're coming home with me, my little spitfire."

"Barbara had it coming," another woman called out over the murmuring crowd. "I'd like to slug her myself."

"Let 'em at each other," someone else said. "Nothing more entertaining than a good cat fight. My money's on the little one."

The manager frantically signaled the band, and they started to play. Grudgingly Mercy allowed Sam to turn her away from Barbara. She took two steps, then gasped with pain as someone pulled her hair. Hard.

She spun on her heel, cheeks blazing. Barbara smiled and wiggled her painted fingernails. "You witch!" Mercy cried, starting forward, murder in her deep brown eyes.

Sam jumped between them, holding Mercy off with both hands. "Honey, look at this rationally. You're little and she's big, and those are bad odds. Let's get out of here."

"She pulled my hair!" Mercy tried to go around him, to no avail. A grinning cowboy with a huge handlebar mustache was holding Barbara back while her fingers clawed the air in Mercy's direction.

Suddenly Sam heard the sound of glass breaking. He groaned, watching a beer bottle fly through the air. He was a veteran of barroom brawls from his hell-raising days, and he knew when a situation was past saving. A chair crashed to the floor in the corner, then a table tipped, then the entire room suddenly broke out in a wild free-for-all.

There was no time to lose. Barbara was fighting her way over to Mercy and Mercy was clawing her way closer to Barbara, and Sam didn't want the best thing that had ever happened to him getting her beautiful eyes scratched out.

He moved quickly, picking Mercy up and swinging her over his shoulder. "We're out of here, babe."

"What are you doing?" Mercy's little red boots kicked wildly in the air. "Put me down, dammit! She started this! Where are you going?"

"I'm saving your hide," Sam replied, ducking a flying water jug. "Stop kicking me."

"I don't want my hide saved! She hurt me, dammit. Let me go. *Let me go!*"

Sam started to laugh then. He could hardly walk for laughing. "Never," he managed to say, kicking open the exit door. "Not as long as I live."

Six

"Do you know what happened back there? Do you know what I did? I was the cause of a disgusting, drunken brawl. Little Mercy Rose Sullivan, who has never so much as said 'Boo' to anyone in her entire life. Sweet Mercy Rose, who always tried to keep the peace, who always kept the Golden Rule. Sam . . . I tried to do *bodily harm* to another human being. I incited a riot."

"Yes, you did, honey." Sam reached across the gear shift and patted her leg. "And that nasty old Barbara was a lot bigger than you too. Don't let anyone ever tell you that you aren't a feisty little thing."

"Sam, I'm serious!" Mercy couldn't believe he was deriving so much amusement from the whole thing. She could have been killed. He could have been killed. She'd never been exposed to people who jumped into a bar fight as if it were a nice refreshing swimming pool. She was still shaking. "Don't you realize what just happened?"

Sam pulled onto the highway, glancing into the rearview mirror. He could see the flashing lights from the police cars approaching from the opposite direction. "I do realize what happened. We got out of there in the nick of time."

Mercy slumped down into her seat, an expression of utter misery on her face. The window was cracked three or four inches in deference to her claustrophobia, giving her overheated skin a brisk cool-down. "I turned into an animal."

"You're being a little hard on yourself, don't you think? You never even hit anybody. Neither did I, come to think of it. We behaved ourselves pretty well, under the circumstances."

"I wanted to rip every hair out of her head."

"I think the feeling was mutual," Sam replied, passing a slow-moving bus. His hand went to her shoulder and rubbed gently. "She didn't like you much, either."

"You don't get it, do you?" Mercy turned her head and looked at his profile, serene and stunning in the yellow light from the dash. "You don't seem to grasp the *enormity* of what I did. I became violent. I completely lost it!"

"Lost what?" Sam asked mildly.

"My . . . my . . . composure," she sputtered, for lack of a better word. "I'm always composed. I never let my feelings out like that."

Sam nodded thoughtfully. "So how did it feel?"

"How did what feel?"

He glanced at her, a slow smile teasing the corners of his mouth. "Losing it, baby. How did it feel?"

For a moment she studied him, the pale flowing hair, the blue eyes turned to silver in the shadows, the amused curve of his lips. How did it feel? she asked herself.

She realized that it had felt absolutely marvelous.

Her blood had boiled. Her heart had hammered in her chest. Primitive feelings had stirred and snarled inside her. She hadn't worried for a single second about what Sam might think of her, or what anyone else in the bar might think. She had watched that sloe-eye Broadzilla put her hands on Sam, and her anger had detonated in a righteous and highly satisfying blaze of holy hell. It had felt bloody *fantastic.*

"I've never done that before," she said in an entirely different tone. "I was always so worried about what everyone else was feeling, I never stopped to consider what I might be feeling."

"Tonight you were feeling jealous," Sam said with smug satisfaction. "I want you to know, I was very touched. Scared as hell you were going to get your cute little nose broken, but touched."

"Stop the car," Mercy said suddenly.

"What?"

"Stop the car, quick."

He didn't think it was a good idea to argue with a woman who had just discovered the joy of hand-to-hand combat. He turned the Jeep into a narrow residential street and pulled up to the curb. He faced her, one arm stretched along the seat back, the other looped over the steering wheel. "I stopped the car, oh spunky one. Now what?"

"Now this," Mercy said.

She flung herself toward him with a seizure of need, her mouth blending with his, her arms closing tight around his neck. "*This*," she muttered huskily, dragging her lips over his, slanting her mouth first in one direction, then another. "This, this, this . . ."

Sam was taken by surprise, but not for long. His tongue mated with hers. They strained together in the cramped space, his body arching, hers pressing. The bucket seats were a nuisance, then an irritation, then torture. They struggled to get closer, frustration building, hands grasping, hips pushing. They had to stop before they died of need, but neither of them could. Sam had her blouse undone. His fingers were tugging at the front opening of her bra when she pulled back, cracking her knee against the gearshift. She blinked owlishly as the Jeep was haloed in the apricot headlights of a passing car.

"Not here," she whispered, her lips still tingling, burning.

Sam dropped his head back on the seat, closed his eyes, and gripped the steering wheel with white-knuckled fingers. "You started this."

Mercy fumbled at the buttons on her blouse. Her fingertips brushed her hardened nipples through her ecru-lace bra, and she shivered. Her breasts were incredibly sensitive, full and aching. She felt like something sweet and ripe and juicy—a peach, fresh off the tree and hot from the sun. "It's my new motto," she said in a luscious, drugged voice. "Go For It."

He turned his head, smiling at her with passion-glazed eyes. "Oh, I like that motto."

"I used to have another motto—Healthy Cowardice." A long pause followed. How could she explain to him the unexpected relief of finally acknowledging her own feelings? She'd spent so many years of her life as a "pleaser," a woman who loved others more faithfully than she loved herself. What a sad mistake she had made, for herself, for Tucker. She had so nearly missed the opportunity to discover the woman named Mercy Rose Sullivan. And what a surprising, emotional, gutsy woman she was turning out to be. "I wouldn't recommend that motto to anyone. You miss too much of life."

Sam looked at her for a long moment, thoughtfully, assessingly. He reached out his hand, gently smoothing her tangled hair behind her ears. "Mercy . . . about tonight . . ."

The simple touch of his hand flooded her with heat. "What about tonight?"

"I knew there was a chance of something

like that happening. Not the cat fight"—he smiled faintly—"but the interruptions and the autographs, the feeling of being on display. I'd love to be able to walk into McDonalds and eat a hamburger and not worry whether or not I have mustard on my chin, or if my zipper is at half-mast, but things haven't turned out that way. The only way I can have any privacy is if I don't go out in public."

She stared at him curiously. "Then why did you take me there tonight? We could have had dinner at home. We wouldn't have been . . . bothered like that."

"Oh, I would have been plenty bothered." Lazy amusement glowed in his eyes. He wanted to take her in his arms again, but he couldn't, because he knew he'd passed the limits of his self-control long ago. "I wanted you to understand what you were getting into. I wanted to be completely honest with you before we . . . you know, before . . ."

Now it was Mercy's turn to smile. Imagine, the infamous Rebel Without a Pause at a loss for words in a romantic moment. Who would have thought? "Before what?" she asked, wide-eyed and innocent.

He exhaled his breath impatiently. "Well, I don't want to toot my own horn, but I can promise you I've learned to make the most of my private moments. I know there are drawbacks to living in the public eye, but . . . it's not all bad, Mercy. It's something you adjust to eventually."

He stared at her with an earnest expression

more suited to an anxious teenager than a grown man. Mercy smiled tenderly, adoring the uncertain boy within the sophisticated man. She leaned forward, her mouth cool and soft against his in a kiss that was hardly a kiss. "Thank you," she whispered.

Sam rubbed his forehead against hers, his hands stroking the glossy strands of her hair. "For what?"

"For being you. For caring about me. For knowing me better than I know myself. For dragging me out of the bar tonight so I didn't get arrested. For being such a wonderful kisser. For all the thrills and chills. For—"

"I'll get a big head," Sam said, kissing the tip of her nose. "You'd better stop now."

She pulled back slightly, the playful light in her eyes fading. "But you didn't let me thank you for the most important thing."

"Which is?"

She touched her fingers to his parted lips and whispered, "Thank you for giving me the most beautiful night of my life."

He gave her a peculiar look. "We had dinner and started a barroom brawl. That's not exactly the stuff dreams are made of."

"You don't understand." Her smile held more sweetness than he could have explained in a lifetime. She settled back in her seat and fastened her seat belt. When she was certain her voice was going to do what she wanted it to do, she added quietly, "I was thanking you in advance."

Sam couldn't take his eyes off her. He felt

humbled and desperate and joyous with need. His heartbeat became quick and uneven, and he picked up her hand to kiss her fingers.

"You're welcome," he said. "In advance."

The didn't speak another word on the drive home. Neither did they look directly at each other, since they were already attuned to every sigh, every movement. Her entire awareness was focused on him, and his on her. As he followed her into their apartment building, her back burned. She could feel his gaze, hear his thoughts . . .

When they emerged from the stairwell, the first thing Mercy saw were the flowers. Roses, roses of every color in the rainbow, dozens and dozens tied in bunches with huge satin ribbons. They were piled in front of her door like a giant welcome mat, filling the hallway with a delicate perfume.

"Sam . . . they're beautiful!" She knelt down, pulling a single blossom free and rubbing the petals against her cheek. "I've never seen anything like this. You shouldn't have done it."

Sam stood behind her, his hands pushed deep into the pockets of his leather jacket. "I didn't."

"What do you mean, you didn't?" She laughed up at him, but soon lost her smile when she saw his expression. "Sam . . . ?"

"There's a card tucked in there. Why don't

you read it?" He paused, then added tonelessly, "The suspense is killing me."

She swallowed hard and reached for the
card, pricking her finger on a thorn as she
pulled it free. She read it . . . but not aloud.
"Oh."

"Oh?"

She dropped the rose and the card and
stood up. "I'll just leave the flowers out here.
With any luck, someone will come along and
steal them."

"They're from Tucker, aren't they?"

Mercy nodded, staring at him and sucking
on her injured finger.

Sam stared right back, feeling incredibly
vulnerable in his strained and sensitive state.
Silence vibrated between them. "And the
card?" he asked finally, wondering if he really
wanted to know the answer. "What did it
say?"

His expression was closed, guarded. She
wanted to reassure him, but she was too
dammed-up with feeling to find the right
words—old feelings, new feelings, nagging
leftover feelings. The entire night had been
one overwhelming sensation after another.
And now this. *Damn* Tucker and his blind,
stubborn persistence. "It doesn't matter,
Sam. Tucker has nothing to do with us. I
don't want to think about him.

"Well, he didn't give you much choice, did
he?" Sam bent and picked up the card. The
message was short but to the point.

I'll be in Denver Friday. Stop fighting me, love.

Tucker.

"At least he's not waiting downstairs," Sam said after a long pause. He looked up at Mercy, an odd smile curving his lips. "Mommy always told me every cloud has a silver lining."

"There's no cloud over us." Mercy kicked at the flowers, making a path to the door. "Just a tangle of soon-to-be-dead roses at our feet. Besides, now I'm forewarned. I'll have to play hide-and-seek again next weekend."

As he walked behind her into the apartment, Sam realized he still held Tucker's message in his hand. While Mercy was busy turning on the lamps in the room, he tore the card in half, then stuffed it in his pocket. It didn't make him feel any better.

He sat down on the edge of the sofa, preparing to say something tender and romantic to recapture the mood. What actually came out was, "Good old Tucker has incredible timing, I'll say that for him."

"Sam—"

He threw up both his hands. "I'm sorry, I'm sorry. I won't say another word about him. I won't even mention his name."

"Thank you." After a moment's hesitation, Mercy sat down beside him. Her thighs were an erotic weight against his, and her shoulder brushed his arm. The silence was awkward.

"Tucker," Sam said suddenly.

Mercy's head bobbed and swiveled. "What? Where?"

He stood up, walking over to the fireplace mantel. There was a framed photograph he hadn't noticed before. A man in a New York Yankees uniform, complete with dimples, curly hair—the whole shot. Mr. All-America. "Isn't this Tucker?"

Mercy walked over to the picture and slammed it facedown on the mantel. "I don't know why I kept that stupid picture anyway. Maybe to remind me what a lucky escape I had made."

"You didn't tell me he was a baseball player."

"It didn't matter. Tucker is ancient history."

"And he plays for the Yankees?"

Mercy sighed deeply. He wasn't going to let this go. "Yes, he plays for the Yankees. Is there anything else you would like to know?"

Sam stared at her, then turned and braced his hands on the mantel, one knee slightly bent, shoulders taut with strain. He didn't want this night to come apart at the seams because of a pretty-boy baseball player named Tucker, but he couldn't seem to stop it. There were things he had to know before he put his heart on the line. "How long have you known Tucker . . . what's his last name? I forgot."

"Healy." Mercy went to him, circling his waist from behind, resting her cheek on the cool leather of his jacket. "I've known him since I was about ten years old. We grew up in the same neighborhood."

Ten years old, Sam thought numbly. Which

meant that Tucker had been part of her life for almost fifteen years, whereas Sam had known Mercy for . . . what? . . . four days? Four days to fifteen years. Those were very bad odds. "And how long were you engaged?"

She sank against him, holding him tighter. "Eighteen months. Sam, why do we have to—"

"I don't know why. But we have to. Why did you leave him?"

"I got tired of forgiving him."

He turned to face her, his hands closing over her upper arms. "Other women?"

"That was part of it. Other women, the rumors about the road trips, the dates he never showed up for . . . Tucker always thought he could get away with anything if he was charming enough. And he was right, until I finally had the courage to leave him and start over."

Sam felt a soft heat of anger flooding his chest. What a fool this Tucker had been. Sam had spent the last ten years of his life searching for someone like Mercy. The few eager, unstable relationships he had had never led him anywhere, just back, and back again, into the maze of loneliness and longing. Eventually it had become easier to be alone than to be disillusioned. The circles he traveled in were dominated by self-centered men and women who made vows they had no intention of keeping and bore children they never saw. Sam didn't want that, but he never saw any proof there was anything more. And so he'd waited, hoping one day he would find someone to fill the curious emptiness in his spirit.

And while Sam had waited, Tucker Healy had used and abused the love of a lifetime.

Sam closed his eyes and drew Mercy close, folding her into his arms with all the tenderness he was capable of. He rubbed his chin on the top of her head, his hands moving in shaking circles on her back. "It isn't fair," he said, very softly. "The way things are in this world, the tender hearts that get bruised and broken, the cold hearts that survive. I'm so sorry, Mercy. He should have cherished you. I would have, I swear I would."

The unvarnished sincerity in his voice tore at her heart. Her vision became blurred and stinging. "What about your heart?" she whispered, nuzzling her face between his open jacket, finding the movement of his heart against her cheek. "Has it been broken too?"

Sam wanted to say no . . . until he pulled back and saw the twin tears rolling like diamonds down her face. She was crying. The tears were for a man named Tucker who didn't deserve them, but she was giving them as freely as she had given her love for so many years. Sam took a hard breath, reality whispering along his raw nerves like hoarfrost. He backed away from her, wondering if the anguish inside him was visible on his face. Quietly he said, "Not until tonight."

"Sam—" Her voice broke. She was overwhelmed by what was happening between them. It was all going so wrong, so horribly wrong. "This doesn't change anything."

He held her gaze as the anxious tenderness within him all but begged him to take her in his arms and kiss the tears from her face. But something held him back. There was still unfinished business between Tucker and Mercy—he saw it in her eyes, he felt it in the very air around them.

"I have to go," he said. "I'm sorry."

Mercy shook her head. "Why?" she whispered helplessly.

"I keep thinking . . ." He tipped back his head and stared at the ceiling, trying to find logic in his tangled emotions. "I keep thinking about the way you left him. You were running from him. People don't run unless they're scared. And you're planning to keep on running, aren't you? I can't help but wonder what you're so scared of."

She crossed her arms around her waist, as if turning to herself for comfort. "I don't understand. I don't understand why you're doing this."

His expression didn't alter. "It's hard to explain. Whatever you're still scared of . . . I'm scared of too." He turned away from her, and all the while he wanted to go to her, hold her.

But his needs came second to hers, and he knew they always would. This was why hearts get broken, he thought, understanding for the first time in his life. You couldn't protect yourself when you were compelled to protect someone else first. He wasn't the one she needed. Her tears told him she was still grieving for Tucker, still vulnerable to him. "I'm sorry, baby. Three in a bed is one too many."

"I only see two of us," she whispered.

Sam went to the mantel and righted Tucker's picture. "Funny. I see three."

"Do you?" she asked, even more softly. "Then I guess there's nothing more to be said. I won't beg you to believe me."

I wish you would. But he didn't say the words, because that wouldn't be fair, either. Was Mercy turning to Sam . . . or running away from Tucker? Sam was terribly afraid she didn't know the answer herself. All he could do was give her time to try and understand her own mind. He'd never been a man who could wait, but for Mercy . . . he would have to learn.

Damn, he wished he hadn't seen her cry.

He shoved his hands in his pockets and walked to the door, deliberately avoiding her eyes. His self-control was only so tempered. He had stopped praying that he would handle the situation with finesse. At this point, it was all he could expect of himself to handle it at all.

"You're limping," Mercy said suddenly.

Sam paused in the open doorway. "There must be a storm coming." Token words, devoid of emotion, filling a painful silence that made him want to bury his fist in the wall. "I told you I had bad knees. They always go stiff when a storm is coming."

Mercy spoke through a hard breath. "Sam . . . this is crazy. Why are you leaving?"

He thought about his answer carefully. He stared at the floor, his wide mouth quirked in a sad smile. Then his blue eyes lifted to hers. "Why am I leaving? Blame it on guilt, fear, demented chivalry . . . but the truth of the matter is, I'm leaving because I love you." He shrugged helplessly. "I love you with all my heart."

Her steady gaze grew brilliant, almost wild. Her chest lifted and fell against the light blue fabric of her blouse, and her face flooded with heat. Sam Christie loved her. He loved her.

He searched her stunned dark eyes, and his smile warmed slightly. "Poor baby. You weren't expecting that one, were you? I'm sorry I'm not more . . . eloquent. Good night, Mercy Sullivan."

Seven

It started to rain around midnight.

Sam wasn't sleeping, he hadn't even taken off his clothes. He was pacing his apartment like a caged lion and trying not to think. He tried not to think about Mercy and the fact she was only a short elevator ride away. He tried not to think about Tucker, because the man irritated the hell out of him. He tried not to think about this coming Friday, when Tucker-who-irritated-the-hell-out of-him would be in town. Who knew what would happen Friday? Not Mercy. Not Tucker. Not Sam. He felt as if he were trapped in a game of musical chairs, with three people, two chairs, and no promises.

He had to get out. He threw on his leather coat again, not really caring that the rain would ruin it. He gave up the elevator for the stairs, not because he was claustrophobic, but because he had energy to burn. On the fourth-floor landing he paused for a quick-breathing moment, his teeth clamped together so hard he thought he would crack a filling.

He'd never needed anyone the way he needed Mercy Sullivan.

He walked the streets, anonymous and silent as the sky poured down on him. His hair was matted to his head, beads of water clung to his eyelashes. He gave up the struggle not to think about Mercy. This was a night for brooding, for brooding like hell, as Tommy Evans the photographer would say. Memories collected and lingered in his mind . . . Mercy standing against a sun-filled window in her ridiculous pink pajamas . . . Mercy sitting in a bog of swamp water and laughing until she cried . . . Mercy with her eyes spitting temper, her hand pulled back in a mean little fist . . .

His knees were killing him. He stopped and sat on a park bench beneath a dripping elm. Directly across the street was a lighted phone booth. He stared at it, thinking of all the things he wanted to say to her, all the things Tucker had already had a chance to say to her. Fifteen years of intimacy bound Tucker and Mercy together, years filled with bright hopes, bitter disappointments, smiles, and tears. It wasn't fair. He'd only had four days. Tucker had had practically a lifetime.

Sam had always been a man who loved to win. He had taken every advantage, worked every angle, given 110 percent of himself and then given more. Once he knew what he wanted, he went after it with every fiber of his being. He knew without a shadow of a doubt that he wanted Mercy Sullivan, but he wasn't accustomed to going into a fight as the underdog.

Four days. They had laughed, they had argued, they had played . . . but never once had they slept in each other's arms. Never once had he possessed her body, filled her with pleasure, taken her to the limits of her control and beyond. His heart constricted in his chest as he wondered how many times Tucker had done that for her.

No, he didn't like the odds. Sam was a gambler, a man who had once promised one hundred million Americans a gold medal while his fingers were crossed behind his back. He hadn't really minded taking the risk, since he knew he was evenly matched with the other athletes. At that point, it was just a matter of who wanted it the most.

This was altogether different. He had deliberately walked away from Mercy, leaving her to sort out her own feelings. But what if his noble and selfless gesture had been a bit premature? He still had three days before Tucker arrived, three days that should have been his, *theirs*. He looked at the telephone across the street and a slow, whimsical smile lighted his eyes. Seven days with Sam Christie as opposed to fifteen years with Tucker Healy.

Yeah. That should balance the scales pretty evenly.

He fished two quarters out of his pocket, and walked over to the phone booth. He called Information, then dialed the number they had given him for Mercy Sullivan on Brockbank Road.

She answered midway through the second ring. She was wide awake, he thought with satisfaction, and it was nearly two in the morning.

"I can't sleep," he said.

"Sam? Is that you?"

"It's me." A courageous gesture, calling the woman he loved at such an unholy hour, but the next step was harder.

"You sound funny . . . I can't hear you."

"I'm at a pay phone." I want you, I need you. . . .

"Are you all right?"

"Yes . . . no." He closed his eyes, his fingers tight around the receiver. "I'm not all right."

"What did you say? You sound all fuzzy."

"That was thunder." She sounded so far away. "Mercy . . . I was wrong. I need you tonight. We need each other."

There was a long, crackling silence. Finally, just when Sam thought he would die of the uncertainty, she said, "The door's open."

He heard the longing in her voice, and his heart began to pound slowly in his chest. Very gently he hung up the receiver, but a smile curved his lips as he sagged against the glass wall of the booth.

He hadn't finished talking to Mercy Sullivan—not by a long shot.

She was wearing her pink pajamas again.

She thought of changing while she waited for him, but the only really nice nightgown she had was made of peek-a-boo lace and not much else, and might be a little obvious. So she brushed her hair until it crackled and dabbed some perfume between her breasts and sat down on the sofa with her heart in her eyes and her eyes on the door.

He didn't knock, and he didn't bother to ring the bell. He just walked in, the way she knew he would, and took her up in his arms. They stood in the center of the room, rocking silently together, holding the moment as long as they could. She didn't care that he was dripping wet and that her pajamas were soaked. Holding him was everything, knowing that he needed her as much as she needed him. His face rested against her neck, his hair was cold and sleek against her cheek.

"I love you," he said quietly, the words barely more than a whisper. "I would never hurt you, Mercy."

"Yes." She tipped her head back and touched his face. "I know."

He saw that she had been crying. Her eyes were faintly swollen, her damp lashes tangled together. He wanted to know who the tears had been for, but he didn't ask. This night was for healing, for loving. Tomorrow was a risk he was willing to take.

He would only ask one thing of her. He cradled her face in his palms. "Remember this night," he whispered. "Whatever happens, promise me you'll always remember."

"I promise." Her voice was throaty, a husky temptation. Her hands slipped beneath his jacket, then beneath his sweater. Her touch was warm on his cool skin, her fingers moving in slow erotic circles over his back. She heard the sharp intake of his breath, could feel the suspended sexual longing in his body. "I want to touch you everywhere. I want to know everything about you. I want to become part of you."

His beautiful mouth tipped in a shaky smile, his eyes full of sensual heat. "You will." His pulse became a slow, uneven rhythm as he bent his head to hers, his tongue stroking provocatively against her lips until they parted on a sigh. Then he held nothing back, dragging her closer, his hand on her nape as he kissed her with all the love, all the passion he was capable of. His tongue played in and out of her mouth, working magic, his love open and flowing to her like a deep, hidden spring. The low throb he felt inside became almost painful, but he deliberately ignored it. At this moment, he only wanted to give—to give to her forever and always, the best things, the sweetest things . . .

But Mercy had gifts of her own. She took his

hands and placed them on her breasts over the pink cotton, staring at him with heavy-lidded eyes. "Feel my heart?" she whispered. "It's beating so fast. You do that to me. No one has ever made me feel pleasure the way you do."

His gaze darkened as his fingers slowly began to massage her breasts. The material was damp, sticking in patches to her skin. "I've made you wet."

Her head tipped to one side and her eyes closed dreamily. "Uh-humm."

"Does this feel good?"

"You . . . you know it does."

"And this?" He caught one tiny-hard nipple between his teeth. He tugged gently, gently . . . then his lips began to drink from her, suckling through the wet fabric.

Mercy's hands closed convulsively over his sweater, catching fistfuls of the soft knit as spasms of desire knifed through her. She wanted to be still, to concentrate on *feeling*, but she couldn't. Her hips arched, her legs trembled. Agonizing, wonderful minutes later he leaned away to look at her.

"I'll be so good to you," he said. "It's all I ever wanted, Mercy. From the moment I first saw you, it was all I wanted."

She clung to him, her face tight against his. She was deaf to her own words, but he heard her whisper: "Take me to bed. I'll be good to you too . . . I'll be so good to you."

Breathless, she rode in his arms to her bed. They shed clothes without reservation, tumbling on the bed like children at play. But they weren't children, they were a man and a woman starved for each other, and the need that had tormented and delighted them from the beginning had finally taken control. She rolled with him, tangled in bedcovers, trying to find all the ways she could fit against him. She nuzzled, she pressed, she curled into him, her small hands learning the power she had over this man. She discovered where to touch, when to caress and tease, and when to stop teasing. The passion knocked the breath from her body.

They talked, but in gasping, disconnected sentences.

"Yes . . . there . . ."

"More . . ."

"Love you . . ."

"Oh, please . . ."

Sam gave as he had never given in his life, mindlessly and joyfully, making each sensual discovery last as long as he could. He was stunned, then delighted by her willingness to do anything, to try anything. Her body was his, all his, and he could do with it what he wished. She turned and lifted and opened at his urging, anxious for his heady caresses on her hot body. Yet he held back, invading her only with gentle fingers, wet tongue, sweet lips. He made her smile, he made her cry out in need, he made pleasure tears sparkle in her passion-drenched eyes. She was cherished, body and soul.

Sam knew he was pushing his endurance to

the limit. He was only a man, and he had never wanted a woman so much. Abruptly he sat up on the bed, pressing her back against the pillows while his thighs parted her legs. He held his body above her, poised and trembling, while his eyes reminded her of her promise.

Remember this.

He sampled her swollen lips one more time, then slowly eased himself down, down to the soft, hot, dewy places that were so anxious to receive him, places he had prepared with love and patience. She shuddered as he entered her, his hips coming against her slowly, so slowly. He thrust deeper, until he filled her completely, his eyes drifting closed and his ragged breath catching in his throat.

Mercy braced her shaking hands against his shoulders. The tension she felt beneath her palms was incredible, steel beneath silk. She was overwhelmed with a fierce desire to have more of him, and she arched her back, teeth bared. He was so warm and hard within her . . . nothing had ever felt so good. She thought she would die with the pleasure of it.

But there was more—so much more. He began to move within her in a languorous, skillful motion that kindled a soft cry from her. It was an exquisite, nerve-racking rhythm, increasing at such a maddening pace, she began to writhe and twist beneath him. But he held her down with his hands, his eyes blazing into hers, muscles shivering and straining.

"Sam . . . I can't stand this. . . ."

"Yes, you can." His voice was hoarse, but his gaze was infinitely tender as he stared down at her. "This and more. It can be even better. . . ."

Then, with a breathtakingly sensual smile, he rolled over on his back, remaining within her as she sat astride his thighs. Watching her face above him, he saw her eyes widen and her mouth part as she instinctively eased herself more tightly around him. His hands were on her hips, guiding her sweetly into movement. Their rhythm synchronized gradually, the small of his back undulating, her body pushing and ebbing. He closed his eyes, giving himself up to the sweet oblivion of her body merging with his, giving himself to the explosion of sensation that met every thrust. Unknowingly his arms reached above his head, hands closing tightly over the brass headboard, the muscles in his arms straining and pulsating.

And Mercy . . . Mercy saw his face below her in a blurred way, saw the hot colors on his cheeks and the tumbled halo of his hair. His eyes were closed. She wanted to see his eyes. She slowed her movements for an instant, her laughter a ragged shiver as he threw her a look of bright blue frustration. She started moving again, meeting his hips with fierce intensity, holding his gaze as they plunged into a rhythm they were powerless to control. Her hands were fists on his shoulders, her heels dug into the bed. She had never known such pleasure, or such pain. She had to find the end of it. She was wild and wet, strung out on passion, drifting into a heady delirium. She was aware of nothing but him, then suddenly she was aware of nothing but the first faint pulsations.

He knew the instant she began to peak. He had kept that much of himself in control, waiting until she was poised at the brink of her climax. He groaned, changing positions with her in a spare, skillful movement. His first plunge was deeper, deeper than ever before, and the pleasure sharpened for both of them. He was filled with love, but driven by a lust that was beyond anything he had ever known. His hands grasped her hips, lifting her to meet his demands. Finally he had given all he had to give. Now he wanted, needed, plundered, questing as fiercely as a hunter after his prey. Dimly he heard Mercy's cry of astonishment, then of joy. Her pleasure triggered his own, and he gave a sound between a moan and a growl as he reached the summit of a devastating physical release.

Still gasping, Mercy felt him holding back for an interminable moment, then he came against her so hard that her hips dragged along the mattress. He called out her name as a shuddering reaction gripped him, his head thrown back, the veins in his neck corded like whips.

"Sam . . ." Her voice was almost silent. What they had shared was a miracle to her.

He fell across her breasts, and her arms

immediately closed tight around him. She held him and stroked him as she would a child, and she wet his hair with her tears.

And Sam kissed the tears away, knowing this time they were tears of joy.

They lay curved together in the dark beneath a heavy patchwork quilt, the way two lovers do when passion is spent. Neither of them could sleep, although it was nearly four in the morning. They were both conscious of time as they had never been before. They were greedy for every minute.

Her head was on his chest, and his hand stroked her hair, again and again, with a gentle, loving rhythm.

"This answers one question, anyway," Sam whispered softly.

She snuggled against him, hooking her leg over his knee. "What question?"

"What it is I've been looking for all my life."

She became quite still, then raised up on one elbow and regarded him gravely. Her eyes held a liquid radiance, her tousled dark hair a ravished sheen. She could hardly speak for the fresh tears that burned her throat. "Me?"

He had to smile at her incredulous tone. "Yes, my love. You."

She took a shuddering breath, her pulse skipping a pair of beats. A full minute passed before she found her voice.

"I love you."

Sam's eyes widened slightly, speared with

moonlight. He hadn't realized how much he needed to hear those words from her. He touched her cheek, quietly savoring his jubilant emotions. "Thank you."

Her watery chuckle tickled his chest. "No. Thank *you*. Thank you for the most beautiful night in my life. In advance."

He raised one brow, his fingertips stroking her nose and lips. "In advance?"

"Well, there's tomorrow . . . and the day after that. You know." Mercy snuggled into the comfort of his arms, her palm warm over his heart. "I'll just keep thanking you in advance, and you'll just have to keep outdoing yourself."

Sam threw one arm over his head. "It's a good thing I love a challenge." He was silent for a moment, then he pressed a kiss on the top of her head. "Mercy? Did I ever tell you about my home?"

"The potato farm? No. I'm not sure I believe it, anyway."

"It's true," he said. "I grew up on a farm in Idaho, smack dab in the middle of nowhere. The nearest house was twenty miles away, the nearest town fifty miles. I had an hour-long bus trip just to get to school and back again. I nearly went *crazy* growing up. That's why I loved skiing. I could tear down that mountain at sixty miles an hour, and I felt as if somehow I was *going* somewhere. I kept looking at my parents and wondering how the hell they went on day after day in that place, always smiling, always content. But now . . ." He turned his head, looking out the window, staring at the same moon he had stared at so many times as a child. This night, however, it didn't look nearly as far away. "Lying here with you in my arms, I finally understand. They had everything life had to offer all along. They still live there. They get up at dawn and eat together in the kitchen, they work side by side, they sit in the porch swing and hold hands like teenagers in the evening. And in the winter . . . in the winter they play Scrabble in front of an applewood fire and laugh themselves silly. I'm . . . happy for them."

Mercy closed her eyes, love for Sam flowing through her clear and bright. She clung to him, and her words were whispers between the kisses she scattered on his neck and face. "Sam . . . you're so . . . you are so . . ."

"So what?" His mouth found hers, initiating a deeper contact. "I am so . . . ?"

She rolled on top of him, her smile enlarging the single word. "Loved."

Eight

Mercy was very, very late getting to work the next morning.

Her eyes were heavy, but her smile was drowsy and sweet and permanent. She had three phone calls before noon, all from Sam, all for no reason but to tell her he loved her. Finally she explained to him that she loved him very much also, but he was going to get her fired if he kept calling. Did he want to get her fired?

Yes. Then they could move to a potato farm.

No. She was a city girl. Was he still sore in that unusual place?

Maybe a little.

Poor baby. That was the price he had to pay for being the Rebel Without a Pause.

Such a funny girl. He wouldn't call anymore— that day.

True to his word, Sam obligingly changed

tactics. Three hours later a wheelbarrow full of white daisies was delivered to Tommy Evans's studio. The accompanying card invited Mercy to a candlelight dinner at Sam Christie's residence that evening, eight o'clock, black tie, black lace underwear optional.

Judith snatched the card out of Mercy's hands and read it, then dropped like a stone to the sofa in the reception room.

"You and Sam Christie . . . Sam Christie and you . . . black lace underwear—"

"The underwear is optional," Mercy pointed out with a sleepy smile.

Judith shook her head as if thinking was almost more than she could handle under the circumstances. "Well, I have to say . . . I don't know what to say. The man is a celebrity. I saw him on a television talk show last week. He's on the cover of a magazine this month. He's doing a movie with Tom Selleck—"

"He's what?" Mercy asked, momentarily diverted. "He never said anything about a movie."

"Well, that's what I heard." There was a long pause while Judith stared intently at Mercy. "Dear, I have to ask you this, for your own good. Did you know about him and that centerfold model?"

"He's never met her. That was just a rumor."

"You're sure? Did he tell you that?"

Mercy nodded, rolling her wheelbarrow to the far corner of the room. "I'll leave these flowers by the potted palms here. Tommy will never notice them. I have to get back to work, Judith."

"Well, aren't you going to tell me *anything*? Is he wonderful? Are the two of you serious? Do the soles on your shoes melt when he kisses you? Do you realize you are the most fortunate woman in America? Aren't you going absolutely crazy waiting to see him again?"

"Yes," Mercy said.

Sam could have hired a caterer to handle the dinner. Instead he chose to cook it himself. A truly romantic evening called for a personal, hands-on approach.

Halfway through the hollandaise sauce for the asparagus he decided the hands-on approach might have been a mistake, at least as far as the food was concerned. The sauce was scorched on the bottom, watery on top, and smelled like rancid cottage cheese. Sam dumped it down the sink and opened a can of cream of mushroom soup to serve as sauce. You couldn't go wrong with cream of mushroom soup.

By seven-thirty he had managed to dirty every pot and pan in his once-spotless kitchen, clog up his disposal with artichoke leaves, and set off his smoke detector three times. Still, the table in the dining room looked impressive, even if he did say so himself. The tablecloth was clean, the candles stood almost straight in their holders, and the wineglasses were free of water spots. The drapes on the sliding door leading to the balcony were pulled back, giving a spectacular view of the city. Sam set the stereo to playing softly and turned the lights down low, mentally rubbing his hands together in gleeful anticipation.

He would see her soon, another thirty minutes . . .

Since the affair—so to speak—was black tie, he took great pains with his appearance. In the last few years he had acquired several tuxedos, but only one he felt truly comfortable wearing. It was cut on simple lines, with a plain white dress shirt free of ruffles and tucks and all the other frills that made him feel like a Ken doll whenever he wore them. For the first time in his life he tried to take a blow dryer to his own hair and make it look really nice, but he only succeeded in creating a thick head of static. He wet it down and combed it in his usual haphazard style, then sat down on the couch in the living room to wait.

At five minutes to eight he realized he had put on his brown Loafers with his tuxedo. He raced to the bedroom to change, then back out again in stocking feet when he thought he heard a knock. When he opened the door, the hallway was empty. He returned to the bedroom, giggling like a schoolboy. By the time he had his dress shoes on, he was laughing, every bit of him buoyant with joy. No wonder his parents had such a great time playing

Scrabble. The smallest things took on a whole new meaning when you loved. Cynicism was impossible. Boredom was unthinkable.

Again he sat on the sofa and glanced at his watch. One minute to eight. It was Tuesday. His smiled faded and heartbeats ripped up into his throat. Three more days . . .

Until what? he asked himself. Mercy loved him. Tucker wasn't going to change that, whether he was there or halfway across the country. No one was going to change that.

Don't think.

A knock sounded, and he stood up as if someone had shocked him, smoothing his jacket, straightening his bow tie. He walked over to the door and opened it, then promptly forgot how to breathe.

He'd never seen her in a dress—and he'd never, ever seen a dress like the one she had on. There wasn't much to it, just a sparkly tube of rich, deep purple that cupped her hips and left her shoulders and beautiful legs bare. She wore long fussy earrings that brushed her shoulders, and her hair was a mass of tumbled curls, swept to one side.

"Hi," she said softly, tilting her head slightly, her earring glinting in the fluorescent lights. She affected a bedazzled, self-conscious expression, rocking back and forth on her high heels. "I was wondering if you would give me your autograph, Mr. Christie. I'm a big fan of yours."

Sam nodded, holding the doorknob for support. "You can have my autograph. You can have . . . anything . . . you want."

"In that case"—She gave him a saucy smile as she walked past him—"I'd better come in. This could take a while."

Sam swallowed hard and shut the door. When he turned back to Mercy, she had dropped her cover-girl composure, standing in the middle of his living room and staring at him with dark, needy eyes. He took a step forward, then muttered, "Oh, baby . . ."

Before either of them realized what was happening, they were in each other's arms, kissing and gasping love words and kissing some more. He was careful of the dress—she looked so pretty, and he thought it might fall off easily. He kept his hands on her back and in her hair, lifting up the silky strands and letting them fall back through his fingers. He hadn't expected to lose control quite like this, but neither had he expected the loneliness that had eaten him alive throughout the day. She was like a powerful drug to him. Addiction at first sight.

"I'm getting all messed up," she murmured, not really caring. "I wanted to look so nice for you."

His tongue traced the outline of her lips. "You do, you do . . ."

"I didn't have any black lace underwear . . ."

"That was a joke . . ."

"So I didn't wear any underwear at all."

He closed his eyes and groaned. He tried to put her away from him, but she came right back as if she were on springs. "Mercy, I've reverted back to an oversexed teenager tonight. We have to be . . . you have to take it easy on me. Be nice."

"I am nice," she murmured kicking off her shoes one at a time, raising up on her bare toes to brush a butterfly kiss on his lips. "See? Wasn't that nice?"

"Mercy, I have a rib roast cooking . . ."

She giggled, rubbing up against him like a sleepy kitten. "Sam Christie, I do love you. Will you take me in the bedroom and make mad, passionate love to me?" She lowered her voice to a husky plea. "It's been eleven hours since . . . you know."

Sam sighed deeply, surrendering himself to the lifeforce of this amazing, delicious woman. "Eleven hours? I hadn't realized it had been so long. You poor girl."

"You poor boy."

"We could always eat later."

"We could eat now *and* later," she said ingeniously.

They kissed their way into the bedroom. A single lamp cast soft white shadows in the corner of the room. He picked her up and set her gently on his bed; when he would have joined her, she pushed him off with a hand on his chest.

"Brood," she said. "Take off your clothes and brood like hell."

He straightened slowly, staring at her. "*What*?"

"All right, you don't have to brood." A smile

shaped her moist lips as she leaned back on her elbows. "Just take off your clothes. And thank you . . . in advance."

He looked wary. "For what?"

"For taking them off *verrry* slowly."

"Let me get this straight." His gaze traveled the length of her, taking in her slim, shapely body, lingering on the tight little skirt that had ridden to her thighs. "You want me to put on a show for you?"

She shook her head, the very picture of wide-eyed sincerity. "No, my love, my dear, sweet Sam. I want you to take off your clothes for me . . . one at a time. Pretend we're playing strip poker and you keep losing. After all . . ." Her fingers plucked at the clingy material of her dress, pulling the bodice down to heart-attack level. "The only thing I'm wearing is this itty-bitty dress of mine. I can have it off in no time."

"I see." Sam walked around the bed at an unhurried pace. Little Mercy wanted to play games, did she? A smile flickered to life as he shrugged out of his jacket and dropped it carelessly on the floor. "Well, whatever you want, honey. I'm not exactly Chippendales material, though."

"The bow tie," Mercy whispered, stretching out her legs and crossing them at the ankle. Her toes were tingling.

"The bow tie," Sam echoed. He took it off with one hand, staring at her with heavy-lidded eyes. "Do you give tips?" he asked, tossing the strip of material on the foot of the bed.

"Not until you get down to your Comfort Weave underwear." Mercy's voice sounded a little strained. It was amazing how arousing the simple act of taking off a bow tie could be. "You know, my boy, I think you have a real talent for this sort of thing."

Sam's face had taken on an intent, drowsy look as he stared at her, never blinking, never looking away. "I have other career plans." He undid his cuffs, then worked on the buttons of his shirt one by one. The shirt drifted open, revealing a finely muscled chest and taut stomach. His hot blue eyes held utter deviltry as he shrugged it off.

"Mercy," Mercy whispered, feeling a twist of longing so intense, it was actually painful.

"You know what?" He stepped closer to the foot of the bed, his hands going to the waistband of his slacks. "I think I'm having an attack of shyness. I'm going to need some help here."

She knelt on the bed, her trembling fingers touching the intoxicating hollows of his ribs. Slowly her hands moved lower, to his zipper. She pulled it down an inch or two, then her arms dropped limply to her sides as she stared at him. "I can't. This is making me crazy."

"Good," Sam said, finishing the job he had started in one swift movement, kicking the slacks aside. He went down to her like hot wax, removing her dress while he held her and stroked her and kissed her. Her body was warm, so warm and welcoming, knowing the comfort and the joy he could give. The teasing foreplay had put him on the brink; he tried to hold back, but she was slipping her legs over his shoulders, arching up to meet him. He buried himself within her with a desperate cry, exulting as her hunger and impatience matched his. He realized that her fragility disguised a hidden strength, that she needed this fusion of their bodies and souls just as much as he did. He rained a waterfall of kisses on her lips and face and hair, not caring where he gave or received. She took him in with every powerful thrust, then asked for more. Even as they sought release, they fought against it, clinging to the razor-sharp edge between agony and rapture. When at last the inevitable came, they were helplessly enmeshed with each other. Her pleasure was his and his was hers, and together they followed a fiery path to a breathtaking, sweet destination.

They had tuna sandwiches by candlelight. The smoke detector went off twice while they ate. The smoke from the burned roast was still hanging in the air, despite the windows Sam had opened. Sam tucked a nice warm blanket around Mercy's shoulders to ward off the chilly breeze. Neither of them had bothered to dress formally. Beneath her blanket, Mercy was wearing one of Sam's oversize T-shirts and a pair of woolen socks. Sam had donned his favorite terry cloth robe, then added the black bow tie for a touch of class. They drank a fine wine with their tuna sandwiches.

"It's too bad about your knees." Mercy sighed, idly running the tip of her finger around the rim of her wineglass. "If you didn't have bad knees, you could join Chippendales. You'd be wonderful at all that dancing and bumping and grinding."

"Change the subject," Sam muttered. "You're embarrassing me."

Mercy looked at him in delight. The man whose body had made Comfort Weave underwear famous was blushing like a Boy Scout. "You never cease to amaze me, Sam Christie. I keep looking for signs of that cocky rebel you used to be, but I just don't see it. Do you know, I saw you on television when you gave that interview before you skied in the downhill? I remember you had pierced ears and hair to your shoulders, and you smiled into that camera and said—"

"'I'm bringing home the gold,'" Sam finished, shaking his head. "Wasn't I something back then? You'd have to look far and wide to find someone as egotistical and presumptuous as I was. Let's change the subject again, okay?"

"It's hard for me to believe that was you. You're so sweet, so unassuming . . ."

Sam grinned. "What I am is thirty-four years old. As far as professional skiing is concerned, that's over the hill. About four years ago, I faced the fact I was due to retire. I'd won the World Cup, but only by the skin of my teeth and the grace of cortisone shots. It's hard to feel like the cock of the walk when you're a *retiree*."

Mercy happily studied his beautiful face, from hairline to chin. "As far as I'm concerned, you're still the cock of the walk. And if you didn't have bad knees, you'd make a terrific Chippendales dancer."

"Thank you," Sam said, "but I do have other plans. I'm negotiating with a sports network to do color commentary for the professional racing circuit. Once the deal is in the bag, I can eat lots of pizza and stop working out and never worry about what I'll look like with my shirt off." He smiled and stroked her jaw with a knuckle. "It's a more *dignified* way of making a living, don't you think?"

Mercy leaned forward, kissing him with lingering sweetness over the remains of her tuna sandwich. "I think you are the most sexy, adorable, *talented* retiree I have ever fallen head over heels in love with. And I would like to thank you. In advance."

He chuckled weakly, rubbing the tip of his nose against hers. "Oh, no. Lady, you're going to kill me."

"No, no, no . . . I'm not going to be unreasonably demanding on your poor over-the-hill body. I want to invite you to go away with me for the weekend."

Sam lost his smile. He sat back in his chair, regarding her with quiet eyes. "Do you?"

"I've never been to a ski resort," Mercy said. "We could drive to Aspen. I know it's spring, but it would be fun, anyway. We can hike around the mountains and you can tell me all your old cock-of-the-walk stories, just like a good retiree should. What do you think?"

Sam dropped his head against the back of his chair, staring at the ceiling. It was a long time before he spoke. "I'll tell you what I think. I think Tucker Healy is coming into town on Friday. I think you'd rather play hide-and-seek than face him."

She didn't quite look at him. "Tucker has nothing to do with this."

"Oh, yes he does."

"All right." Mercy spoke evenly, smoothing the tablecloth with her fingertips. "I don't want to argue. It was just an idea. Forget I said anything."

He raised his head, staring at her. A small muscle ticked in his jaw. Suddenly there was an air of furtiveness about her, and he hated that she wouldn't look at him. "Answer one question for me, Mercy. What are you frightened of?"

She pulled the blanket closer around her shoulders. "I'm not frightened of anything. I thought it would be nice to spend the weekend with you, that's all."

Sam felt a moment of panic, but he quickly subdued it. He still had three days, he told himself. He would take them one at a time, making every waking moment as rich and full and satisfying as it could possibly be. He couldn't envision a fairy-tale future with Mercy while Tucker still had this hold over her, so he wouldn't think about the future at all. He wouldn't.

The hell he wouldn't.

He stood up abruptly, blowing out the candles. "Come back to bed."

"Sam . . ."

He looked down at her. His eyes told her everything his pride and his fear wouldn't let him say. "I need you, Mercy. Tonight I need you to be good to me."

In the shadows of the room, his eyes were soft, his hair a rainbow of white and gold, his face heartbreakingly open to her. There was a rustle of movement as she stood, pressing herself close to him, holding him tight.

"I'll be good to you," she whispered, feeling his broad back tremble beneath her palms. She was overwhelmed with the need to pleasure and soothe and comfort him. "I love you, Sam. I love you so much."

And for the space of one more night, they danced with dreams.

Nine

Mercy studied the face of her lover in the soft
morning light. Sam Christie was breathtaking in the unguarded dishevelment of sleep.
His ruffled hair was tangled with sunlight, a
warm flush stained his cheeks below his thick
gold lashes. His mouth was slightly parted,
and the undefended expression on his face
made her smile and kiss the top of his head
ever so lightly. He was a dear, beautiful
man—he had given her so much in such a
short time. Not only passion, but the sweet
preludes to passion she had never experienced before: laughter . . . a few tears . . .
daisies enough to fill her arms to overflowing . . . and so much understanding.
She still felt his hands, his kisses, his legs
tangled in a lover's knot with hers. She would
have liked nothing better than to wake him
with sleepy kisses and whispered love words,

but reality was shining brightly through the bedroom window. The Cinderella ball was over, and it was time to face the day. It wouldn't be wise to be late for work two days in a row.

Her heart broke a little as she left Sam in his bed and crept down the stairs to her apartment. She had the feeling her heart would always suffer a pang or two when she left him, regardless of the circumstances. Her mind kept going back to tender places, warm memories. And she found herself craving brand new memories, anxious to have this day finished with so she could have more and more of him. She felt as if she were missing out on the constant feeling of surprise whenever they were together. How hard it was to pretend she was like other women, content to go off to work and try to think and see and do in a responsible manner. She wasn't like any other woman. She was Sam Christie's woman, and that fact made her very special indeed. She knew she would never be completely comfortable without him by her side. She missed him already. At the door of her apartment she nearly turned and ran back up the stairs to tell him so.

But it was eight o'clock, and Tommy Evans was not famous for his forgiving nature. Mercy showered and changed into a black cashmere T-shirt and khaki slacks, then spent five minutes rifling through her bedroom for her black Loafers. She was on her stomach searching beneath her bed when she heard a knock at the front door.

Sam.

Laughing, barefoot, Mercy ran for the door. The poor man had probably been distraught when he had opened his eyes and found her gone. He probably needed a little good morning kiss to give him strength to face the day without her.

She flung wide the door, a huge, puppy-dog grin on her face. "I'm so happy you . . ."

Tucker Healy was smiling at her, one hip propped lazily against the door frame. "I'm happy to see you too, Cookie."

Mercy stared at him in stunned disbelief for perhaps ten seconds before she could do anything but shake her head. His eyes were just as green, his smile the same one that had lived in her dreams for so many years. "Tucker," she whispered. Then, with an embarrassing squeak in her voice, "What are you doing here?"

"I got tired of chasing you. I told you I was arriving on Friday to make sure you would be here on Wednesday." Without invitation he walked past her into the room, looking around with bright-eyed interest. "Nice place. I especially like that picture on the mantel."

Mercy cursed herself for not having thrown Tucker's picture out with the trash. Her mouth dry with anxiety, she slowly closed the door. "You shouldn't have come. There's nothing for you here, Tucker."

Taking his time, Tucker walked over to the

window and looked outside. Then he turned to face her, sitting on the edge of the sill, arms crossed over his chest. He was wearing a forest-green shirt that matched his eyes, rolled up to the elbow. "Brat," he said with careless amusement. "You've gotten pretty independent living way out here by your little lonesome."

"You're right," Mercy said flatly. "I have. And the last thing I need in my life right now is you."

"Really?" He locked gazes with her, and his smile widened. "If you're so independent, why is your face the color of cottage cheese? You can't expect me to believe you don't have any feelings for me."

"Believe what you want. I really don't care." She needed all her concentration to speak calmly. She wanted to run, she wanted to hide, she wanted to go back upstairs in Sam's bed and toss the covers over her head. For so many years, Tucker had held such sway over her emotions. Deep inside, she burned with panic. She couldn't escape the irrational fear that he still had the ability to turn her life topsy-turvy. Tucker's name had always been synonymous with upheaval and uncertainty. "It's over, Tucker. I told you that when I left New York, and I meant it."

"Did you?" Tucker's expression had never been sweeter, more sure of its power. "I think you needed a little time by yourself. But it's been nearly two months, Mercy . . . more than enough time for both of us to realize what's really important in life."

"You're so right." Mercy hid her hands behind her back to hide their telltale shaking. "And believe it or not, I finally do have my priorities in order. And you know what? You're not at the top of the list anymore, Tucker. You're not even *on* the list."

Tucker raised his eyebrows and whistled softly. "So little Cookie has grown claws. All right, I guess I deserved that. I don't blame you for wanting a little of your own back. I realize I hurt you. I'd cut off my arms before I'd ever let that happen again."

"Don't be so rash with your promises, Tucker." Mercy was feeling incredibly light-headed, and she realized she'd locked her knees together. She sat down on the sofa, taking a deep breath and hunching her shoulders against the chills in her spine. And next on the agenda, she thought dismally, would no doubt be the ever-popular hiccups. "If you cut off your arms, you couldn't pitch anymore, could you? You couldn't lift a beer mug, you couldn't dance with all the pretty girls who ask for your autograph. No, I wouldn't make a promise like that. Let's be practical. Say something like, 'I'd cut off my hair before I ever hurt you again, Mercy.' That's a promise you can live with. Your hair will always grow back."

For the first time, uncertainty flickered behind Tucker's eyes. "Mercy, this isn't like you. You've never shut me out this way."

"You're wasting your time, Tucker. Go home."

He stood up slowly, walking toward her with a "try and make me" smile she recognized only too well. "But I just got here. Why would I want to go home?"

He was reaching for her when a soft knock sounded at the door. Before Mercy could move, Sam opened the door and walked in. He was smiling—until he saw Tucker. He stiffened visibly, his gaze flicking to the picture on the mantel and back again. The expression on his face said that he'd received better surprises in his life. "Christmas came early this year," he said.

Mercy stood up in an awkward rush, feeling like a puppet with tangled strings. "Sam . . ."

"Sam?" Tucker echoed, his eyes narrowed.

"Yes, *Sam*," Mercy shot back at him, feeling her nerves fraying at the edges. "Don't look so surprised, Tucker. We're not engaged any longer. I don't owe you any explanations. I don't owe you anything."

"Isn't this an interesting development?" Tucker murmured, walking slowly around the sofa and holding out his hand to Sam. "I recognize you. Sam Christie, right?"

Sam felt an involuntary movement clutch his stomach muscles as he briefly took the younger man's hand. "Right. And you must be Tucker Healy. Mercy has spoken of you."

"Has she?" Tucker looked at Mercy and his tone dropped. "So you've made friends with the famous Sam Christie. You're full of surprises, aren't you, little girl?" Then, to Sam he said, "I heard you retired from professional skiing a couple of years back."

"That's right." Sam's lips twisted in a smile, but the tight, withdrawn expression on his face didn't change. "Almost four years ago."

"Must be a bummer, checking out of the fast lane. *Retiring*. Hell." Tucker shook his head and shrugged. "I know I'm not looking forward to it. Of course, I've got at least ten good years of playing ball before I have to worry about anything like that."

Not if I toss you out of the window in the next five seconds. "That's real nice," Sam replied tonelessly, inwardly seething with frustration. He should have had three more days with Mercy before Tucker invaded their lives. Damn, damn, damn, damn, damn. Why was it the devil always kicked you hardest when you weren't looking? "Mercy tells me the two of you grew up together."

"That's right." Tucker smiled at Mercy, who stood like a statue in the middle of the room. "We've always been pretty tight. Matter of fact, I've been real lonely without her these past couple of months. I flew out to Denver hoping to convince her to spend some time with me."

"I told you," Mercy said quietly. "You wasted your time, Tucker. We have nothing left to say to each other."

"That's a real shame." Tucker's sparkling green eyes caressed her from head to toe. It was the look that had always worked in the past. "And here I've come all this way just to see you. C'mon, Mercy. Can't you spare a couple of hours to have dinner with an old friend? That's all I ask, just a couple of hours."

Mercy felt as if a jackhammer were going off in her head. Nothing about this scene felt real. There was Tucker, playing the irresistible boy-next-door role to the hilt, intimating that all he needed was a couple of hours to win her back. And Sam . . . everything about him was folded up, closed tight, locked away from her. She felt a quiet chill shiver through her as she looked from one man to the other. At the moment, she didn't feel capable of getting through to either one of them. "Tucker, I told you. I can't see you. Sam and I are—"

"Actually, this might work out after all." Who had said that? Sam thought to himself. Had it really been his voice, so friendly and controlled? Amazing what a man in love was capable of. "That's what I came down here to tell you," he went on, lying to Mercy with an apologetic smile. "I'm afraid I have to go out of town. Business. Some of the big boys at the network want to discuss my new contract. I'll be gone several days, so you'll have plenty of time to spend with Tucker."

Mercy stared at him. This was the last thing she had expected. Why wasn't Sam helping her? Why wasn't he making things easier for her? "You're not . . . leaving?" she asked hoarsely, trying to tell him with her eyes how much she needed him.

"'Fraid so. I don't have any choice." His

heartbeat was fast, too fast. He knew he was hurting her, and there were no words to describe what that did to him. Still, it had to be kinder than the torture of pulling her in different directions. He wouldn't help her hide, neither would he beg. He would only love her, and hope. "I'll be back Sunday or Monday. That should give you two plenty of time to . . . catch up on things."

Mercy drew a sharp breath, feeling frost growing under her skin. "Then that's that," she whispered. She felt lost, angry. Suddenly everything was torn apart, nothing was the way it should be. The one sure, dependable thing in her life had evaporated in the blink of an eye. Like it or not, she was left to see this thing through on her own. She tossed her hair back, hardly seeing the smug expression on Tucker's face as she smiled at him. "I guess that answers your question. Dinner tonight?"

"Perfect," Tucker murmured, looking very self-satisfied. He walked to the door, sketching a brief salute to Sam. "Nice meeting you, Christie. I'll take good care of our girl while you're gone."

Our girl. That almost did it. Sam watched him open the door, his fingers clenched into fists at his side. Amazingly, he managed to keep his cool. "You do that, Tucker."

"Eight o'clock?" Tucker asked Mercy.

She nodded.

He blew her a kiss and shut the door.

The room filled with a flat silence. Sam looked at Mercy. He was anxious to be gone now, before his good intentions went up in smoke. He took a moment to study her face, the lost, dark eyes, the sweet, vulnerable curve of her cheek. She had never been more dear to him—or more distant. "My plane leaves in an hour." He was showing quite a talent for improvising under stress. "I need to pack. I'll give you a call when I get back. All right?"

"All right? Sure, that's just—" She broke off, trying to swallow. Her voice was a thread of sound as she finished, "Just fine."

He would have kissed her, but she pulled away, looking at him with teary confusion. He drew back, the ghost of a smile on his lips. "I'm not abandoning you, love."

Stubborn in her trauma, she said softly, "Oh, really? That's what it feels like to me."

"You're wrong," he said. "This isn't good-bye, Mercy."

"Well, I know it can't be hello. You tell me it isn't good-bye—just what is it, Sam?"

"It's . . ." He gave a bitter laugh, his calm beginning to slip. "It's one of those painful middles." He turned, limping slightly as he walked toward the door. Another storm coming, he thought. The pain seemed to spread from his legs to his chest, pooling in his heart. He didn't dare look back at her. He had no idea what expression was on his face.

"Take care," he said, closing his eyes briefly

as he opened the door. "Take care of your-self."

"I don't have much choice, do I?" Mercy whispered bitterly.

She felt nothing.

She dressed for her date with Tucker automatically, drawing on fifteen years of familiarity. He liked the color blue. There was a blue dress in her closest she hadn't worn since she'd left New York. She didn't like it, but Tucker had always complimented her whenever she had worn it. She curled her hair with hot rollers that burned her scalp, and spritzed herself with the perfume he had given her for Christmas. It was amazing how easily she slipped back into the old routine without giving it a thought.

There was such an emptiness inside her. She missed him. Sam . . . her friend . . .

She applied her makeup more heavily than usual. Red lips. Red cheeks. Deeply shadowed eyes.

Where was he now? What was it like for him right now?

She put on shoes with uncomfortably high heels. They went with the dress she hated. She put on the earrings that went with the dress she hated. She looked at the clock and saw that it was five past eight. Tucker was always late, but she imagined this night he wouldn't be as late as usual. He was trying too hard.

She walked past the floor-length mirror in the bedroom, then stopped in her high-heel tracks. She backed up slowly, a sharp frown cutting through her brow as she studied her reflection.

Who was that woman?

She looked like a Bunny, or a Dee-Dee . . . or a Cookie. All soft and fluffy, a delicate little thing who wobbled slightly on heels that were much too high for her. Her eyes looked twice as big with all the makeup, eating up her pale, heart-shape face. She was vaguely familiar to Mercy, a stranger she had once known and never really liked. She took absolutely no pleasure in knowing that Tucker would approve of that stranger wholeheartedly. It wasn't Tucker's opinion that mattered to her. Not anymore.

Mercy sat down hard on the edge of the bed. There had been a time when her desire to please Tucker had been her overriding emotion. If he liked her dress, if he liked her hair, then she was acceptable. If he found fault with her, she was responsible. It had been such a relief to put some distance between them, to finally have the freedom to please herself. Sam had once asked her what she was afraid of. Now the answer was suddenly so clear that she gasped. She had assumed she was only free of Tucker if they were separated. And that may have been true, for a time. But no longer. Her eyes watered, but not with tears. Her heart gave a twinge, but it wasn't really pain. It was a vague sorrow for this too-late, guilty man.

Mercy stood, taking one last look at herself in the mirror. "Will the real Mercy Rose please stand up?" she murmured, a smile flickering to life inside her. "You have a date tonight, sweetie. It's time to get ready."

Tucker arrived at half-past eight. Mercy Rose Sullivan greeted him at the door, startling him into dropping the armful of roses he carried.

"Good grief," he said, looking her up and down with an expression of stunned amazement. "I said eight o'clock. Why aren't you ready?"

Mercy shrugged, pushing back the brim of her baseball cap. "I am ready, Tucker. I didn't feel like dressing up tonight." She was wearing her red boots, soft blue jeans, and a white cable-knit sweater that came halfway to her knees. She grinned as she noticed Tucker's gaze frantically searching for her breasts beneath the bulky material. "What's the matter?"

"What's the matter? You look like a Boy Scout, that's what's the matter. What's gotten into you?"

"What's gotten into me?" she repeated thoughtfully. "What a good question, Tucker. *I've* gotten into me. You asked to take Mercy Rose Sullivan to dinner, and Mercy Rose you get. I felt like wearing jeans tonight. I felt like putting my hair in a ponytail. These boots are very comfortable, and so is the sweater. I like this hat too. I think it makes me look kind of cute. I realize you can't see my cleavage, but into each life a little disappointment must fall."

Tucker walked into the apartment, throwing his flowers on the coffee table. His expression was that of a sulky little boy who was being forced to eat broccoli for dinner. "Okay, Cookie. You've made your point. You're wonderfully independent, and you dress to suit yourself. Now go put on a nice dress and I'll take you out. I've starving."

But Mercy had another point to make. She walked up to Tucker, nose to nose, her small hands closing like vise-grips around his shoulders. "I have something to tell you, Tucker. I hate the nickname 'Cookie.' I always have. Don't ever call me that again. I am not a *Cookie*. My name is Mercy Rose Sullivan, and I thank God it isn't Mercy Rose Healy."

Tucker shook her off, looking around wildly, as if he might have stepped into the wrong apartment. "I don't get this. Everything was fine when I left here this morning. Now you've turned into . . . you've turned into . . ."

"Me," Mercy said emphatically, shaking her ponytail. "What do you think of me, Tucker? Not that it really matters. I like me. I would be happy to go out to dinner with you, but I'm not taking off my baseball cap, and I refuse to put on a smidgen of lipstick. I'm not in the mood."

"I'm not taking you anywhere looking like that," Tucker said flatly. "You've played your little game long enough, Mercy. Drop the act and change your clothes, or else."

It was a showdown, Mercy realized, feeling her fighting spirit tingle to life. "Or else *what*?" she asked, dark eyes sparkling with anticipation.

"Or else I'm leaving, and I won't be back. I don't think either of us wants that."

She smiled brightly, tipping her baseball cap back with one finger. "Actually, Tucker, that's exactly what I want. I don't know what you want any longer, and I really don't care. I'd very much like to send you off to the airport and stick a frozen dinner in the microwave."

Tucker stared at her, a flush streaking his cheeks like slap marks. "You don't mean that."

He looked so stunned, Mercy couldn't help but feel sorry for him. Beautiful Tucker, who would no doubt break foolish, trusting hearts till the end of his days. But not hers. Never again hers. She touched his face one last time, a shaky smile curving her lips. "I'm afraid I do," she said softly. "Go home, Tucker. I can't be what you need me to be. I've given up too much for you already, all those years when everything I did was motivated by guilt and fear. I'm not willing to do that any longer. I've finally discovered that it's possible to love someone without giving up yourself in the process."

"Sam Christie?" His face grew pale with anger. "What you're really trying to say is that you found someone who can give you more than I can. He's quite a feather in your cap, isn't he, Mercy?"

She dropped her hand. "I suppose you would see it that way," she murmured sadly. "I'm sorry it had to end like this."

"Yeah," Tucker said with a sneer, chucking her under the chin so hard it hurt. "I can see that your little heart is broken, *Cookie*. When it all falls apart around you, don't come running to me. I don't give second chances."

"I already found my second chance," Mercy said. She walked to the door and threw it open, standing aside to let him pass. "Goodbye, Tucker. I hope you find whatever you're looking for."

He flashed her a barbed smile. "Don't worry about me. I look out for number one."

He walked out without a backward glance. Mercy shut the door quietly, feeling the emotion-charged room settle into calm. "Isn't that the truth?" she whispered.

And then she thought of Sam, and the sparks of sadness faded from her eyes. She'd made it through this "painful middle" with flying colors, thanks to him. Her heart soared in her chest like a bird on the wing. There was an incredible feeling of freedom that came with facing life squarely, something she had only had glimpses of until now. How much of her newfound courage, her sparkling self-confidence came from the knowledge that

Sam Christie loved her as no man had ever loved her before? She wondered. What other man would have walked away, leaving her alone to discover her own strength? Oh, she needed Sam. She needed him more than she had ever needed Tucker Healy, but not to fight her battles or slay her dragons. She needed him to share her life, two hearts and two minds intertwined. He'd known that all along. He'd just been waiting for her to catch up with him.

She ran into the bedroom and flopped full-length on the bed. Her hat tipped down and covered her face and she giggled beneath the brim, remembering Tucker's expression when he had walked in the door. Horror.

"The man doesn't know what he's missing," she said. She pulled off the cap and tossed it in the air with a war whoop. "Mercy Rose Sullivan, my hat's off to you."

And then she turned on her stomach and propped her chin in her palm. There were plans to be made. Now that the painful middle was safely behind her, it was time to get on with a glorious future. How strange life could be with its sudden twists and turns, how surprising. Unexpected beginnings. Those painful middles. Astonishing possibilities. Such heartache, caused by a man who had turned out to be a stranger after fifteen years. And such joy and love, shared with a dear companion she had met barely a week earlier. Time was irrelevant when it came to matters of the heart. A lifelong friend could be made with a single smile. Bright new dreams came like a rainbow, when you least expected them, and happy-ever-after was more than a fitting end to a child's bedtime story.

Who would have guessed?

Ten

Mercy waited semipatiently for four days, haunting the stairwell between the fourth and eleventh floors, leaving little notes pushed underneath Sam's door. She felt like a Comfort Weave underwear groupie.

By Sunday morning there had still been no phone call. She was getting worried. Sam's giving her space to sort out her feelings was one thing, but falling off the face of the earth was something else. Finally she called the one person in the world she could think of who might know Sam's whereabouts.

Dr. Jack Menzies's answering service informed her the doctor was unavailable, with the smug satisfaction of a banker turning down a loan application. Mercy told them it was an emergency, she was in labor and the pains weren't very far apart. The answering service said they would contact the doctor right away. Less than a minute after Mercy hung up, Jack Menzies called her.

The doctor sounded extremely groggy, and more than a little confused. "This is Jack Menzies."

Mercy glanced at the clock for the first time since she had opened her eyes that morning. Six-thirty. She hadn't realized it was quite so early. "This is Mercy Sullivan. I'm sorry to call so early, but it's an emergency."

"Mrs. Sullivan? I don't recall any patient by the name of Sullivan. See here, I'm an ear, nose, and throat man, and I think you must have confused me with . . ." Silence. "Wait a minute. It's you, the one in the pink pajamas. Mercy. Are you all right?"

"No, I'm going crazy. I mean, yes, physically I'm fine, but . . . look, have you heard from Sam lately? He left town a few days ago, and I haven't heard from him since."

"Oh, I *wish* he'd left town." Jack lowered his voice to a whisper. "Mercy, I promised Sam I'd stay out of this, but . . . four days ago he showed up on my doorstep with his little overnight bag and the saddest story I'd ever heard. He's been staying with me."

"With you? He told me he had business out of town."

"He lied. From what I understand, he was being noble or chivalrous or some such thing. If he'd checked into a hotel, the news would have gotten out pretty quick, and he didn't want you to know he was still in town. It's kind of hard for Sam Christie to keep a low profile. He's sacked out on my couch in the living room as we speak." Another pause. "When he drinks too much, he snores. Did you know that?"

Her heart turned over, and she wanted to cry. "Oh, dear. Is he all right?"

"He's on pins and needles. The Rebel Without a Pause has not only paused, he's stalled. Did you get a phone call last night about midnight?"

"Yes. Whoever it was hung up on me. I thought it was a wrong number."

Jack sighed. "That was Sam. He was missing you. He's not good at being noble, you know. It's killing him."

Mercy closed her eyes, longing in her chest. She pictured Sam Christie dialing her number like a schoolboy, just to hear her voice before he hung up. The tears welled up in earnest now, but they were happy tears. "Jack, when does he plan on coming out of hiding?"

"He 'officially' gets back in town today, praise the Lord. He has a personal appearance scheduled at Pederson's Sporting Goods later. He's going to look like hell too. Mercy?"

"What?"

"He's a good man. Underneath the glitz, the hype . . . he's a real sweet guy. I'd hate to see him get hurt."

Mercy smiled through her tears. Happy-ever-after was getting closer every minute. "He's going to be very happy, Jack. We're going to live on a potato farm together."

"What?"

"A figure of speech, Jack. It's just a figure of speech."

Sam looked like hell at his personal appearance and he knew it. He felt like hell. He'd been eating very little the past couple of days and drinking a bit too much, and his stomach was hosting a three-alarm fire. His knees were also giving him fits, thanks to a thunderstorm that had blown up during the night. He was not a happy man.

He sat behind a teakwood table at Pederson's Sporting Goods, signing autographs and plugging the new line of outerwear that carried his name. The huge store was filled to overflowing, despite the rain that poured steadily outside. He'd been signing his name since noon, and his fingers were permanently cramped around the pen. He'd already stayed the promised two hours. There was a limo waiting for him in the parking lot behind the store, but he didn't have the heart to leave. Some of these people had been there since early that morning, standing outside in the rain to get a chance to meet him. Representatives from the Denver television stations were there as well, and he'd promised an interview after the autograph session.

Besides, if he left, he would have no choice but to go home. If he went home, he was bound to see Mercy. If he saw Mercy, she might tell him something he didn't want to hear. Clumsily, gently, he tried to push her from his thoughts, smiling and chatting away with perfect strangers as if his entire future would not be decided in the next few hours. It was useless. She was there, beneath his hand, behind his eyes, within his heart.

What had happened during the past four days? he wondered. Had his good intentions backfired? He knew when he "left town" that he was taking a calculated risk. He was leaving an open field for Tucker Healy, a man he knew damn well would use every trick in the book to influence Mercy's feelings. It went against the grain for Sam Christie to walk away without a fight, but there was more at stake than his pride. He would pull the moon and the stars out of the sky for Mercy Sullivan, but he couldn't give her peace of mind. That she had to find alone.

While he signed his name over and over, he charted a course of action. If all went well, he would swear off drinking forever, shout his love from the rooftops, dance in the streets, send up a zillion balloons, and go shopping for an obscenely expensive diamond ring. If all went wrong, he would join a monastery. It was always good to have a plan in times of crisis.

"Could I have your autograph?"

Someone dropped a yellow Post-it on the table in front of him. "You bet," Sam said, infusing his voice with an enthusiasm he didn't feel. "Who should I . . ."

That voice. That sweet, ingenious, husky little voice, he thought.

Sam looked up slowly, almost fearfully, his heart doing a triple gainer when he met her gaze. He felt thrilled and stunned and completely at a loss. "Mercy?" he whispered.

She was standing there in front of the line, wearing her cute little baseball cap and shiny yellow rain slicker. Her bangs were all soft and fluffy beneath the bill of the cap, framing eyes as bright as sequins. She nodded and tapped the paper. "That's right. Just make it to Mercy Sullivan. I'm a big fan of yours, Mr. Christie. I absolutely love you." She laughed suddenly, breathlessly. "I really do."

Sam looked at the pen in his hand, at the shaking fingers holding the pen. He tried to think, but nothing came. "Mercy," he said again.

"Do you need me to spell it?" she offered helpfully. "It's just like it sounds. M . . . E . . ."

"I can spell you. It. I can spell it." The look he threw her was a mixture of joy, hope, and exasperation. "I can't believe you're here. I've been going crazy, wondering if . . . wanting to see you, find out—" He broke off, looking at the eager faces surrounding them. "Mercy, can you wait while I finish here? We have to—"

"We don't have all day," someone in the line behind Mercy called out. "Stop hogging him, honey. Give us all a chance at the gorgeous hunk."

Mercy shrugged at Sam, her smile infinitely tender, wonderfully familiar. "I'm terribly sorry. I guess I'm hogging you, Mr. Christie. If you'll give me your autograph, I'll be about the happiest woman on earth."

"You're all right, then?" Sam asked hesitantly, his caution tearing at her heart. "Everything . . . turned out the way you wanted it to?"

Mercy gave him a smile that made the breath catch in his throat. "There was never any doubt. And your trip out of town? Did you enjoy it?"

Sam swallowed hard. "Oh, well . . . sure. No. I mean, you know how cold and impersonal hotel rooms can be."

"I do," Mercy said sympathetically. Then she added, "Sleeping on sofas can be murder too."

"Young woman!" The store manager made his way through the crowd and tapped Mercy on the shoulder. "Be considerate of others, please. Don't hold up the line."

"As soon as I get my autograph," Mercy said. She looked expectantly at Sam. "If you wouldn't mind? Write something like, 'Best wishes to my friend Mercy Rose Sullivan.' That would be really nice. I promise you, I'll cherish this little piece of paper forever."

"My friend Mercy," Sam echoed softly. His dear friend.

His smile was slow in coming, but oh boy, was it worth waiting for. He wrote something on the yellow Post-it, then handed it back to Mercy. She read it, then her startled gaze locked with his. The paper fluttered to the floor.

"You're welcome," she whispered hoarsely. "You're so very, very welcome."

And then the Rebel Without a Pause lived up to his name.

While fascinated, envious, and stunned bystanders looked on, he stood and walked around the table, seizing the sweet young thing wearing the baseball cap in his arms and kissing her with all the swagger and dash of a pirate in an historical novel. Ruthlessly. On the lips. Without coming up for air. And he obviously didn't give a damn who watched him do it.

Women started squealing, jostling one another for the next place in line. Cameras started flashing. Security guards plunged forward through the crowd, looking confused as to who should be rescued from whom.

"What did he write?"

"Who is she?"

"Is he kissing everybody?"

"There's no butting in line, toots."

"Don't they need to breathe?"

"My word, he *really* kisses."

One enterprising female crawled beneath the table and retrieved the little yellow Post-it. She read it sitting on the floor, her hand over her heart. "Omigosh. Omigosh. What a man. I think he proposed to her! This might actually be a proposal!"

An eager reporter quickly shouldered his way through the crowd, microphone in hand. "What does it say? Tell us exactly what he wrote to her."

The young woman on the floor turned her best side to the Channel Five Eyewitness News camera and read aloud, her voice quavering with emotion. "It says . . . 'To my friend and my love, Mercy Rose. Thank you for sharing the next fifty years with me . . . in advance.'"

The crowd broke out in a resounding cheer. Mercy pulled away from Sam and asked, "Is this one of those private moments you know how to make the most of?"

Sam framed her face in his hands. Then he began to laugh, and so did she. They clung to each other for support. He kissed a smile on her soft, swollen mouth. "Lady," he said, "you ain't seen nothin' yet."

THE EDITOR'S CORNER

Nothing could possibly put you in more of a carefree, summertime mood than the six LOVESWEPTs we have for you next month. Touching, tender, packed with emotion and wonderfully happy endings, our six upcoming romances are real treasures.

The first of these priceless stories is SARAH'S SIN by Tami Hoag, LOVESWEPT #480, a heart-grabbing tale that throbs with all the ecstasy and uncertainty of forbidden love. When hero Dr. Matt Thorne is injured, he finds himself recuperating in his sister's country inn—with a beautiful, untouched Amish woman as his nurse. Sarah Troyer's innocence and sweetness make the world seem newly new for this world-weary Romeo, and he woos her with his masterful bedside manner. The brash ladies' man with the bad-boy grin is Sarah's romantic fantasy come true, but there's a high price to pay for giving herself to one outside the Amish world. You'll cry and cheer for these two memorable characters as they risk everything for love. A marvelous LOVESWEPT from a very gifted author.

From our very own Iris Johansen comes a LOVESWEPT that will drive you wild with excitement—A TOUGH MAN TO TAME, #481. Hero Louis Benoit is a tiger of the financial world, and Mariana Sandell knows the danger of breaching the privacy of his lair to appear before him. Fate has sent her from Sedikhan, the glorious setting of many of Iris's previous books, to seek out Louis and make him a proposition. He's tempted, but more by the mysterious lady herself than her business offer. The secret terror in her eyes arouses his tender, protective instincts, and he vows to move heaven and earth to fend off danger . . . and keep her by his side. This grand love story will leave you breathless. Another keeper from Iris Johansen.

IN THE STILL OF THE NIGHT by Terry Lawrence, LOVESWEPT #482, proves beyond a doubt that nothing could be more romantic than a sultry southern evening. Attorney Brad Lavalier certainly finds it so, especially when he's stealing a hundred steamy kisses from Carolina Palmette. A heartbreaking scandal drove this proud beauty from her Louisiana hometown years before, and now she's back to settle her grandmother's affairs. Though she's stopped believing in the magic of love, working with devilishly sexy Brad awakens a long-denied hunger within her. And only he can slay the dragons of her past and melt her resistance to a searing attraction. Sizzling passion and deep emotion—an unbeatable combination for a marvelous read from Terry Lawrence.

Summer heat is warming you now, but your temperature will rise even higher with ever-popular Fayrene Preston's newest LOVESWEPT, FIRE WITHIN FIRE, #483. Meet powerful businessman Damien Averone, brooding, enigmatic—and burning with need for Ginnie Summers. This alluring woman bewitched him from the moment he saw her on the beach at sunrise, then stoked the flame of his desire with the entrancing music of her guitar on moonlit nights. Only sensual surrender will soothe his fiery ache for the elusive siren. But Ginnie knows the expectations that come with deep attachment, and Damien's demanding intensity is overwhelming. Together these tempestuous lovers create an inferno of passion that will sweep you away. Make sure you have a cool drink handy when you read this one because it is hot, hot, hot!

Please give a big and rousing welcome to brand-new author Cindy Gerard and her first LOVESWEPT—MAVERICK, #484, an explosive novel that will give you a charge. Hero Jesse Kincannon is one dynamite package of rugged masculinity, sex appeal, and renegade ways you can't resist. When he returns to the Flying K Ranch and fixes his smoldering gaze on Amanda Carter, he makes her his own, just as he did years before when she'd been the foreman's young daughter and he was the boss's son. Amanda owns half the ranch now, and Jesse's sudden reappearance is suspicious. However, his outlaw kisses soon convince her that he's after her heart. A riveting romance from one of our New Faces of '91! Don't miss this fabulous new author!

Guaranteed to brighten your day is SHARING SUNRISE by Judy Gill, LOVESWEPT #485. This utterly delightful story features a heroine who's determined to settle down with the only man she has ever wanted . . . except the dashing, virile object of her affection doesn't believe her love has staying power. Marian Crane can't deny that as a youth she was filled with wanderlust, but Rolph McKenzie must realize that now she's ready to commit herself for keeps. This handsome hunk is wary, but he gives her a job as his assistant at the marina—and soon discovers the delicious thrill of her womanly charms. Dare he believe that her eyes glitter not with excitement over faraway places but with promise of forever? You'll relish this delectable treat from Judy Gill.

And be sure to look for our FANFARE novels next month—three thrilling historicals with vastly different settings and times. Ask your bookseller for A LASTING FIRE by the bestselling author of THE MORGAN WOMEN, Beverly Byrne, IN THE SHADOW OF THE MOUNTAIN by the beloved Rosanne Bittner, and THE BONNIE BLUE by LOVESWEPT's own Joan Elliott Pickart.

Happy reading!

With every good wish,

Carolyn Nichols

Carolyn Nichols
Publisher, FANFARE and LOVESWEPT